She was weary of the whole thing

"I am telling the truth," she said flatly. *Why do I care what he thinks of me?* she asked herself irritably.

"If only you weren't so beautiful," he muttered. "You could put a spell on any man." She tensed, trying to pull free from his hold as he lowered his head to hers. His hands still held her with a cruel strength but his lips brushed hers with exquisite gentleness. For a moment her mouth was paralyzed under his, but she soon delighted in this strange new intimacy.

Very slowly Sean drew back, his eyes momentarily full of questions, then hard with contempt. "You're overacting darling," he said harshly.

His bitter words ripped away the tenderness of a kiss that for Caroline had been a revelation.

Books by Sandra Field

These books may be available at your local bookseller.

For a free catalog listing all titles currently available,
send your name and address to:

Harlequin Reader Service
P.O. Box 52040, Phoenix, AZ 85072-2040
Canadian address: Stratford, Ontario N5A 6W2

SANDRA FIELD

a mistake in identity

Harlequin Books

TORONTO • NEW YORK • LONDON
AMSTERDAM • PARIS • SYDNEY • HAMBURG
STOCKHOLM • ATHENS • TOKYO • MILAN

Harlequin Presents first edition April 1984
ISBN 0-373-10681-5

Original hardcover edition published in 1983
by Mills & Boon Limited

CHAPTER ONE

CAROLINE saw them before they saw her.

She sat very still in her window seat in the little restaurant, feeling the sun strike warm on her right shoulder and arm, hearing the buzz of conversation and laughter and the subdued clatter of dishes.

The hostess had seated Richard and Lenora so that they were both in profile to her. They were unquestionably quarrelling. There was a petulant droop to Lenora's red lips and irritation in the way she snapped her gold cigarette lighter. As for Richard. . . .

At the first sight of him, Caroline's heart had given the old familiar lurch. But now, as she watched him take out his own cigarettes—how well she remembered that elaborately embossed silver case—and tap one on the back of his hand, his brows meeting in a frown, she found herself wondering how she had ever thought there was strength in that admittedly very handsome face. He was as well groomed as always, his teeth as even and white, his eyes as blue; the difference was not in him but in her. As though scales had dropped from her eyes, she saw with something akin to dismay that his chin had a tendency to recede. Only a very slight tendency, mind you. But it was, nevertheless, a weak chin. And the frown between his eyes would be permanent before long. Not for Richard the outburst of honest anger. No, he was too controlled and too much on his dignity for that. So instead, at the age of twenty-nine, there were lines beginning to score his forehead.

The waitress, a plump, adenoidal girl who had forgotten Caroline's salad and had had to be reminded twice to bring lemon for the tea, plunked the bill down on Caroline's table. 'Get you anything else?'

5

'No, thanks,' Caroline said dryly. The seafood casserole, an unhappy blending of lobster, cheese, and some unidentifiable bits of fish, was sitting heavily on her stomach as it was. She gathered up her haversack, stood up, and without consciously thinking about it, walked across the crowded room. 'Hello, Richard,' she said evenly.

He had been about to pick up his cigarette from the ashtray. His hand with its shiny new platinum wedding band remained frozen in the air. 'Why, Caroline! Er— what a pleasant surprise. How are you?'

'Well, thank you,' she answered composedly.

Richard was never one to be off balance for long. 'I don't believe you've met my wife, have you? Lenora, this is Caroline Travers. A—a friend of the family's, from Halifax.'

Caroline was not going to let him get away with that. Smiling sweetly, she said, 'Now, Richard, you know I was always your friend more than your family's. How do you do, Lenora? But of course, you're both on your honeymoon, aren't you? I do hope you're enjoying yourselves.' This was not very nice of her, since it was obvious she had interrupted them in the middle of a disagreement.

Lenora, whose features and clothes bore the gloss of wealth if no other particular distinction, smiled insincerely, although a calculating gleam in the pale blue eyes told Caroline Richard would undoubtedly be subject to a close interrogation once Caroline had gone. She did not need to worry about Lenora, she knew; the Lenoras of this world look after themselves.

As if to prove her point, Lenora said brightly, 'This is such an attractive little town, isn't it?'

'It certainly is. Although I'd have thought somewhere more civilised would have been more your line, Richard.'

'Our firm is doing an audit for the local fish plant; they're involved in a dispute with the revenue department,' he said stiffly. 'Lenora and I are returning to Halifax tonight.'

'Oh, a busman's honeymoon.' And to think she had once admired that streak of practicality in him!

'And you? Are you on holiday? Are you alone?'

'Yes, I am. I need to get away from it all—the store, my staff, and the mountains of paperwork. And as you know, I'd had a few personal difficulties lately.' A low blow. 'So I'm really enjoying the sun and the sea and the beaches—a beautiful spot.' She included them both in her smile. 'Well, I must be off. Nice to have met you, Lenora. Goodbye, Richard.' She could hear the note of finality in her voice, and it would have been a toss-up whom it surprised more: herself or Richard. 'Oh, by the way,' she added kindly, 'avoid the seafood casserole, won't you? Goodbye.'

She threaded her way through the tables, paid her bill, and was outside in the sunshine again. What the restaurant lacked in culinary skill it more than made up for in location: it was nestled in the woods at the top of a cliff, a steep path leading to the beach below, its view stretching across the sparkling blue waters of St Mary's Bay to the low green hills of Digby Neck. An idyllic, picture-postcard scene, a distillation of all the summers Caroline had spent in the Maritimes since she was a small girl.

But now she gave it only a cursory glance, for she wanted to be long gone by the time Richard and Lenora finished eating. She unlocked the chain around the rear wheel of her racing bicycle, adjusted the haversack on her back, and mounted, throwing her leg over the saddle. The gravel scrunched under the wheels, and then she was on the paved highway again, heading back to the hotel. She rode more or less by instinct, her mind very much occupied by what had just happened, her predominant feeling not pain, or anger, or frustration, but simply relief. Pure, unadulterated relief.

Leaning forward, she pedalled up a hill. A truck

swished past her, enveloping her in evil-smelling fumes, which she scarcely noticed.

She was free, she thought incredulously. Free of Richard and all his charms. Released from the toils of her first real love affair, which had begun so blissfully and ended so disastrously that it had been almost a cliché from start to finish.

She had first met Richard professionally, for she had needed an accountant to set up the books in her business, and he had been recommended to her. They had started dating after that, and everything had conspired so that it was inevitable that she fall in love. The bookstore had just begun to run smoothly, so for the first time in months she had spare time on her hands; Richard was different from anyone she had ever dated before: he was sophisticated and suave, exceedingly good-looking, comfortably off; and his air of detachment, of being always in control, strongly appealed to her, for there were times when she deplored her own impulsiveness and lack of forethought. She had admired the way Richard's brain ruled his emotions, wishing she could emulate it. Because he was her opposite, she fell head over heels in love with him; far too much in love to understand that this was the love affair she should have had at eighteen or nineteen and outgrown by twenty. But at eighteen she had been involved in other things, so that when she was twenty-two Richard was the first.

Dazzled with the sheer glory of being in love, she had ignored a host of tiny signs that should have warned her that trouble lay ahead. That Richard only very rarely told her he loved her she put down to a touching shyness; that he made few physical demands on her to an old-fashioned and adorable chivalry; his reluctance to have her meet his friends she attributed to a need to be sure of his feelings for her, to be certain she was the woman he would marry. *She* had never doubted it for a moment. At work she doodled his name on her scrap pad . . . Richard. Richard Mathieson. Caroline Travers. Caroline Mathieson. And she encircled it all with hearts, wondering dreamily where they would live and how many children they would have. She wanted a son called John and a daughter called Margaret. . . .

And then her house of cards collapsed. At the last minute one evening she had gone to the theatre with a girl friend, and Richard had been there with another woman. When she had spoken to him about it on the telephone the next day, confident that there was a simple explanation, he had dismayed her by telling her he was dating someone else, Lenora Baxter, daughter of the senior partner of his firm of accountants.

'But you can't do that!' Caroline had wailed. 'We're practically engaged!'

'I wasn't aware that I'd asked you to marry me.'

'Only last week you told me you loved me!'

Wisely he ignored that. 'I'm not formally committed to you, Caroline. Consequently I'm free to date whom I please.'

'Richard—you can't! I love you.'

'Please, Caroline, you're making far too much fuss. You and I can certainly remain friends, even if I am seeing Lenora.'

Scarcely able to believe the evidence of her own ears, she stuttered, 'So you can have your cake and eat it, too? No, thanks! If you want to go out with Lenora, you go ahead. But don't expect to date me as well!'

'Very well, if that's the way you want it.' Horrified, she recognised an undertone of relief in his voice; he had got rid of her more easily than he had expected to.

She had slammed the receiver back on the hook and collapsed on the bed in a storm of weeping. The first of several such storms, for Halifax was a small city and it was inevitable she sometimes see Richard. When he was with a woman, it was always Lenora. Their engagement portraits in the newspaper a couple of months later should have been no surprise, but hurt horribly nonetheless; Caroline had gone to New Brunswick to visit her parents last weekend, the weekend of the wedding, and had purposely arranged to be away from the bookstore for at least a month afterwards.

It was not, she supposed, that much of a coincidence that she had bumped into Richard at the restaurant. He had contacts all over the province, and when she thought back, he had once mentioned the business he did in the Digby area. What was strange about it all was the sheer elation of realising she was free of him; it was the last thing she had expected. Dimly she was beginning to understand that she had been in love with love, infatuated by a man who did not really exist and by qualities that were the antithesis of those that guided her life. He *would* marry the daughter of the senior partner—of course he would. It would advance him another step up the ladder, for if he was not hot-blooded, Richard was certainly ambitious. She, mere Caroline Travers, ex-ski champion and owner of a small bookstore, had nothing to offer him. Only, she winced, puppy love. An adulation that must have amused him—or, worse, bored him.

Never again, she thought grimly. It would be a long time before she'd fall in love again, and when she did, she'd be a great deal more careful.

She was going fast enough that the breeze was whipping her hair back from her face, and she savoured the air's coolness. Recklessly she leaned low over the handlebars as she raced down the next hill, exulting in the sensation of speed. A bicycle was a poor substitute for a pair of skis, but it was better than nothing. She had long ago recognised that something in her psyche needed excitement and the edge of danger; she had thought she had found both in Richard, but she had been wrong. Totally, abysmally wrong. So what—or who—would take his place? An unanswerable question, she decided, blithely ignorant of what lay ahead.

She had reached the hotel. Once the private home of a wealthy shipowner, it had a widow's walk and a turret, ornamented shutters on all the windows, and quantities of ornately carved woodwork decorating the many landings, verandahs, and staircases. Its excesses gave it a quaint, Victorian charm, its flower gardens making naïve splashes of primary colour against the immaculate white paint. The hotel's cuisine, fortunately, far excelled that of the restaurant where Caroline had just eaten, and the couple who owned and ran it had managed to combine genuine warmth and hospitality with ruthless efficiency, never an easy task. That the hotel was also expensive Caroline had ignored. She had needed a holiday and a bit of pampering, and she was old enough to know that one normally had to pay for such things.

She parked her bicycle behind the hotel, locking it to one of the ornate gas lamps that edged the pathway, then walked around to the front, a slim, long-legged figure in her brief shorts and top. The lobby was almost deserted, for everyone was down at the swimming pool or the beach at this time of the afternoon. Maybe she'd go for a swim herself: she felt the need for some kind of activity to celebrate her newfound freedom.

Avoiding the elevators, which she disliked with an intensity that approached claustrophobia, she headed down the high-ceilinged hallway to the stairs. She had to pass the women's washroom on her way, the one that was used by people who ate at the hotel but were not overnight guests. The door pushed open as she passed and a young woman came out. Caroline gave her a perfunctory smile and then stopped dead in her tracks, the smile frozen on her face.

The resemblance was uncanny. It was almost like looking in the mirror at herself. The same dark chestnut hair, shining under the electric light. The same heart-shaped face, tilted nose, high cheekbones. Even much the same build. Caroline gave her head a shake, and said, a thread of incredulous laughter in her voice, 'Are we long-lost relatives, do you suppose?'

But the other woman did not answer, neither did she smile back. She had clutched the doorpost, and it did not take much discernment to see that she had suffered a severe shock. Her lips stiff, she finally stammered, 'Who *are* you?'

'My name's Caroline Travers. I'm from Halifax. And you?'

'Gabrielle Cartier from—from Vancouver. I-I can't believe this.' She put a shaky hand to her forehead.

Caroline said sharply, 'Are you all right?'

'I-I feel . . .' Her fingers were trembling.

'Look, you'd better come up to my room for a minute, it's only one flight up,' Caroline urged. 'You don't look well. Anyway, it'll give us the chance to have a chat and see if we can trace any family connections.'

'All right, thank you. I—it's been a shock. Sorry to be acting so stupidly.'

'No problem.'

Caroline's room was at the front of the hotel, with its own pocket-sized verandah that had a view of the shoreline and the calm blue waters of the bay. She closed the door behind them both, pulling out one of the white wicker chairs for her guest and perching on the bed herself after dropping her haversack on the floor. She pushed her dark glasses up on her forehead and for a moment they looked at each other in silence.

The other girl said finally, 'You're a little taller than I am. And your eyes are a darker blue.'

Caroline's ski coach, who had had a bent for the romantic turn of phrase, had always likened her eyes to the colour of a lake at dusk. Richard, more pragmatic, had called them navy blue. Caroline herself was realistic enough to think of them as her best feature; they were beautifully shaped, the lids curving gracefully, the brows dark brush-strokes that deepened the mysterious depth of the irises. She responded thoughtfully, 'Your voice is a little deeper, and you have a slight accent. And,' with a laugh, 'you're far more elegant!' For Gabrielle Cartier was wearing teal-blue linen culottes with a silk shirt, Italian leather sandals in exactly the same shade of blue on her feet. Her toenails were painted scarlet, as were her long, pointed fingernails, while the stone that flashed on her index finger, if it was real, must have cost a small fortune.

'You're here on holiday?' Gabrielle inquired. It was an innocuous enough question, yet there was something in her voice that invested the query with more significance that it warranted.

'Yes, I am.' Caroline smiled again, suddenly remembering her meeting with Richard and the joyous sense of freedom it had given her. 'For a whole month—sheer heaven!'

'By yourself?'

Again that slight over-emphasis. 'Well, yes. But why——'

'Please forgive me.' Gabrielle leaned forward, her blue eyes pleading for understanding. 'You must think me very rude asking such questions, but I do have a reason. I——' She spread her hands helplessly. 'I scarcely know where to begin.'

The diamond flashed in the light because Gabrielle's hands were still trembling. Caroline said quietly, 'Something's wrong, isn't it? Why don't you tell me about it?'

'You're very kind. . . .'

'We could be sisters, we look so alike. Perhaps that's got something to do with it,' Caroline said calmly. Sensing that the other girl needed encouragement, she added, 'You do have a trace of an accent, don't you?'

'French is my native tongue. I grew up in Trois-Rivières.' The long, tapered fingers clasped the arms of the chair. 'I am in trouble—you have guessed that already. When I saw you—saw how much like me you look—you were like the answer to a prayer. If you would, you could help me.' The charmingly accented voice faltered. 'But it is a lot to ask. And despite the resemblance, you *are* a stranger.'

By now Caroline was thoroughly curious, and as was usual with her, discretion flew out of the window at the first hint of a mystery. 'Why don't you tell me what the matter is,' she suggested, trying not to sound too eager, 'and then perhaps I can decide if I can help.'

'Very well, I'll try.' Gabrielle paused to marshall her thoughts, her brow furrowed. 'Two years ago I met a young man named Martin Reilly at Laval University. He was two years younger than me, from an entirely different background, taking philosophy while I was soon to graduate in modern languages. A dreamer, a thinker . . . I am a doer, you understand.' She shrugged in a very Gallic way. 'But you know how it is. We fell in love. He was handsome, gentle, charming, and I allowed myself to forget all the obstacles.' Her lips curved a smile. 'Anyway, it was springtime.'

Had Gabrielle but known it, there was no reason for her to explain why she had fallen in love; had not Caroline done exactly the same thing? 'What happened?' Caroline asked softly.

'For a year we were happy, like two children laughing in the rain. It was during that time that I met Martin's brother. Just one time, but I have never forgotten him.' Gabrielle shivered, her face pinched. 'His name is Sean. He is older than Martin by ten or twelve years and as different from Martin as two brothers could be—a tough, dangerous man.'

'He didn't like you,' Caroline ventured.

Gabrielle nodded slowly, staring down at her beautifully groomed hands. 'He took an instant dislike to me. I cannot imagine why, unless it was the way Martin made no secret of his feelings towards me. Martin wanted to marry me, you see. I believe there is money in the family, so perhaps Sean was afraid I was after that.'

Caroline said indignantly, 'He had no business suspecting anything of the sort!'

'None at all, as matters turned out. That meeting seemed to make Martin all the more determined to marry me, and I soon began to realise it could never happen. We were not suited, we were too different. As gently as I could I tried to tell him this, but he wouldn't listen. He insisted we go away together so that he could make me change my mind. We did go away, to Florida and Louisiana, but it was no good. I knew even more strongly that it would be wrong for us to marry, wrong for both of us. So I broke with him altogether.' She spread her hands and the diamond splintered the light into sharp-edged fragments. 'What else was I to do? I felt it was better to end the relationship rather than allow him to continue to hope.'

At least Gabrielle had had the courage to confront Martin directly ... unlike Richard with Caroline. 'I think you did the right thing. Although it must have been difficult to do.'

'It was. He was—what is the word? Distraught. Saying wild things. Threatening to kill himself. I was terrified ... I stayed around a week longer than I had planned, simply because I couldn't just abandon him, and by the end of the week he seemed more reconciled to the break, a little calmer. So I left. I went to Vancouver and got a job there and settled down into a new life. I missed Martin, how could I not? But I still knew in my heart I'd done the right thing.'

This was not the end of the story, Caroline was sure. 'Did something happen to him?'

Gabrielle glanced up. 'You're very quick ... yes, something happened to him. A friend of mine from Quebec, who had also known Martin, came for a visit in Vancouver. He told me Martin had had a nervous breakdown after I left. He was in a mental hospital.'

'Oh, Gabrielle. ...'

The sleek chestnut head was downbent. 'What could

I do? I hadn't been working long enough to have any vacation time accumulated, and I couldn't afford to quit my job. Nor did I have much money, it had taken most of my savings to get out to Vancouver. And what was the sense of me going to see Martin anyway? I wasn't going to change my mind . . . so I asked André— my friend—to visit him and write me a letter.' She picked at the paintwork on the chair with her fingernail. 'While André was at the hospital he met Sean. Sean had been away, you understand, and had only just returned, to find Martin in hospital. It soon became clear to André that Sean blamed me for everything. Sean said it was my fault that Martin was ill and that he'd make me pay for it if it was the last thing he did. According to André, Sean was beside himself. Never had André seen a man so angry, so bitter and full of vengeance . . . he's here now.'

'Who is?' Caroline said stupidly.

'Sean. I saw him, not half an hour ago, outside the hotel. He must know I'm here.'

'But——'

'I have no idea how he found me. This is my first holiday in ten months, and I've always wanted to come to Nova Scotia—but how could he have known that? Unless he was having me followed. . . .'

'This sounds like something out of a spy novel,' Caroline protested.

Gabrielle smiled crookedly. 'It does, doesn't it? Nevertheless, the facts remain. Sean, who wishes to avenge his brother's illness, is somewhere in the vicinity of this hotel.'

'And what do you want me to do?' Caroline said faintly. She already had some inkling of what it would be, but she wanted to hear Gabrielle say it herself.

'I want you to distract him for me. To act as a——' The other girl frowned.

'A decoy?' Caroline supplied wryly.

'That's the word.' Gabrielle leaned forward, focussing all her willpower on her companion. 'If you could draw him off for only an hour or perhaps two—that would give me long enough to get away. I'll go right to the airport, you see. I don't want to stay here now, I'm too frightened of him.'

'If he thinks I'm you, maybe I should be frightened of him too,' said Caroline in rather a muddled way.

'He would not be deceived for long, he's too clever for that. But I wouldn't need very long. Two hours would be enough for me to get away. Please ... say you'll do it!'

Caroline only hesitated for a second. It would give her a great deal of pleasure to thwart Mr Sean Reilly, she knew. He sounded so arrogant, so quick to judge the motives of others and assume the worst. Gabrielle had acted the best way she knew how, what right did Sean Reilly have to condemn her? Besides, it would be an adventure. 'All right, I will,' she said.

Gabrielle closed her eyes, releasing her pent-up tension in a long sigh. 'I-I don't know how to thank you.'

'So how are we going to do it?'

There was the first hint of laughter in the blue eyes. 'You are a very decisive woman.'

'Well, there's no time to waste, is there? We certainly don't want him to see the two of us together, nor do we want him connecting me with Caroline Travers in Room 210. What does he look like, by the way?'

'He's the most attractive man I have ever seen in my life,' Gabrielle said deliberately.

'Oh.' Not quite the answer Caroline had expected.

'Tall, black-haired, grey, grey eyes—like clouds in a storm. And very sexy.'

Only half joking, Caroline said, 'Maybe you picked the wrong brother.'

'And a personality like a rattlesnake,' Gabrielle added viciously.

'Then again, maybe you didn't. How are we going to manage this?'

'He has already seen me dressed like this. Would you object greatly to wearing my clothes? I'm sure they'll fit you, we're much the same size.'

'You'd better give me your address so I can return them. They look expensive.'

Gabrielle dismissed this with another of her shrugs. 'They are only clothes. A small price to pay for getting clear of Sean Reilly.'

'I'm afraid you won't find anything as stylish in my wardrobe.'

'No matter.' Gabrielle stared out of the window, thinking hard, her whole bearing very different from that of the frightened, tension-ridden girl of ten minutes ago. 'Let's see how best to do it ... how about if you leave the hotel in my clothes and stroll towards the town, perhaps do a little shopping. I'm sure he'll follow you. He's out there waiting, I know he is, because he saw me come in here. There are a couple of restaurants on the main street. I'm sure if you went into one of them, he'd join you. By the time you'd eaten, I'd be well away. And you'd be perfectly safe in a public place.'

It sounded almost too easy. Caroline said thoughtfully, 'I'll wear my dark glasses. That way he won't notice the difference in eye colour.'

'The only trouble is, he may speak to you in French. He's completely bilingual.' For the first time Gabrielle sounded worried.

'So am I.' Her ski coach had been from St Jérôme, and she had spent so much time in the Laurentians that French had become almost a second language to her.

'*Merveilleux!* Then we have nothing to worry about.'

Caroline laughed, for the other's enthusiasm was contagious. 'I feel as though we should have a bottle of champagne to toast our venture.'

'Indeed we should! What shall I wear of yours?'

Caroline opened her closet. 'Slacks? Or a dress?'

'Maybe the blue dress, the cotton one. Your slacks would be a little too long for me, I think.'

Thoroughly enjoying herself, Caroline pulled out her prettiest sandals and a matching handbag. Her voice muffled in the closet, she said, 'I'll touch up my hair with the curling iron, so it'll look more like yours. Would you mind plugging it in for me?'

It took nearly half an hour for the change to be effected, for Caroline had entered thoroughly into the spirit of the escapade and wanted every detail to be correct. While Gabrielle changed in the bedroom, she went into the bathroom and smoothed out her hair to a close approximation of Gabrielle's sleek style, painted her nails, and carefully made up her face. In the meantime Gabrielle had changed the contents of their handbags and they had exchanged addresses in order to be able to return everything.

When Caroline finally emerged from the bathroom, Gabrielle gasped. '*Mon Dieu!* You look exactly like me!'

'I do, don't I?' said Caroline with considerable satisfaction. She took Gabrielle's teal-blue leather bag and swung it over her shoulder. 'There—Mademoiselle Gabrielle Cartier at your service.'

'*Magnifique!*' Gabrielle stood up. 'It is less important for me, but will I do?'

'You certainly will. Although I don't think I ever looked that good in that dress.'

Gabrielle laughed. 'It is hard for us to say the other looks pretty, is it not, for it sounds conceited. Are we ready?'

'I think so. I'm going to leave the hotel and walk to the town, taking my time——'

'I never thought to ask. Do you have a car?' There was an unexpected sharpness in Gabrielle's voice.

'No, I don't have it here, as a matter of fact. My bicycle's out back. Why?'

'I just wondered. In case you need it to get away from Sean. But I'm sure you won't.'

Later Caroline was to remember this question. At the time she merely thought Gabrielle was being a touch over-solicitous. Refusing to be sidetracked, she went on, 'I'll window-shop for a while, keeping an eye on him. And then I'll go into that seafood restaurant, it's supposed to be very good. If he comes in, I'll invite him to join me, and I'll be sure to work my way down the whole menu. That should give you all the time you need.'

'And I'll wait here in your room long enough to be certain the two of you have left, and head in the opposite direction. It's foolproof!'

Caroline glanced at her watch. 'It's past four already. I'd better go.'

Gabrielle said soberly, 'I can never thank you enough for doing this for me, Caroline. You'll write to me, won't you? And I'll write to you, and send back your things. If you like that outfit, I wish you'd keep it. It's the least I can do.'

'That's not necessary,' Caroline answered uncomfortably. 'I was in the mood for an adventure, and thanks to you I'm going to have one. The rest of my holiday will probably seem pretty tame after this.'

'I hope not.' Gabrielle held out her hand. '*Au revoir, et bonne chance.*'

'*A toi aussi.*' They shook hands as though sealing a pact, and then Caroline gave herself one last quick glance in the mirror. She was no longer Caroline Travers, she thought with a lift of excitement. She was Gabrielle Cartier from Trois-Rivières, who had been in love with Martin Reilly, and whose honesty and kindness had been misconstrued by Martin's brother. As she went down the stairs, she wondered if this wasn't some of the appeal of acting: this sensation of being liberated from one's everyday humdrum self to be, if only temporarily, somebody else. Taking a deep breath, she walked out into the lobby.

CHAPTER TWO

THE heels of Caroline's sandals tapped across the polished hardwood floor in the lobby. Behind the dark glasses her eyes flickered from side to side. A mother with two children, obviously just back from the beach. An elderly couple arm in arm. A teenaged boy with a cassette recorder stuck in his belt and earphones on his head, his expression blank. But no black-haired man with eyes like storm clouds. . . .

She opened one of the big double doors and walked out on to the front steps. The sun was still deliciously warm; bees buzzed among the snapdragons and salvias, and from the swimming pool behind the trees came the sounds of splashing and laughter. Caroline walked gracefully down the steps, swinging her hips a little more than she would normally. Down the flagstone path and past the parking lot, where she conquered the temptation to examine all the cars for a black-haired driver. Along the gravelled driveway, shaded by maples and pungently scented pines, to the main road.

Her heart was beating uncomfortably fast. For Gabrielle's sake she wanted their deception to succeed. But if Sean Reilly had not seen her, it would all be for nothing. Maybe Gabrielle was wrong, and he'd left the hotel and gone into town. Or maybe he was looking for her down at the swimming pool or on the beach . . . the possibilities were endless, and what had seemed so simple and straightforward in the hotel room was no longer so.

The main road had a sidewalk with grass verges and a gutter. As Caroline turned right, in the direction of the town, she risked a quick, and she hoped casual-looking, glance over her shoulder. A red sports car was pulling out of the parking lot. The driver was, like herself, wearing dark glasses. His hair was black. It had to be; fair hair or red hair would have shown up against the dark interior of the car.

Without breaking stride she continued along the sidewalk, taking her time, a summer visitor out for a stroll. The street was edged with clapboard bungalows and larger, older homes, many with vegetable gardens and fruit trees. For a few minutes she engaged in conversation with an elderly man picking raspberries, seeing out of the corner of her eyes that the sports car had stopped by the side of the road a few hundred yards away. It had to be Sean Reilly. He did not want to pass her and run the risk of being recognised, so he was allowing her to set the pace.

After accepting a handful of deliciously sweet and juicy raspberries, Caroline continued on her way, passing the library and the town hall, the Baptist and Catholic churches amicably side by side, and the post office. An old-fashioned drygoods store drew her attention; she gazed at the display of fabrics, seeing the red sports car reflected in the window. The driver was parking it against the curb. Even as she watched he got out, straightening to his full height. His hair *was* black. And even though his image was distorted by the glass, he gave an impression of confidence that bordered on arrogance and of physical strength that bordered on toughness. She had seen all she wanted to see. She, the decoy, had lured the prey. Now all she had to do was hold him long enough for Gabrielle to make good her escape.

When she came to a clothing store, she went inside and tried on a pair of jeans, and then a pair of man-tailored red shorts that looked marvellous with Gabrielle's silk shirt. Impulsively she bought them both; partly because she wanted them, partly because it seemed to add verisimilitude to her role of casual, unsuspecting holidaymaker. The bag under her arm, she went outside again, looking around her vaguely as if trying to decide what to do next.

He was not in sight. For a moment she panicked, then she saw that the red car was still parked down the street, and forced herself to calm down. He was obviously waiting for the right moment to confront her, and it was up to her to present him with that moment. But not yet ... every minute counted, and she was not sure how long she could maintain her role once they were, for instance, seated across from each other in a restaurant.

Fortunately there was a bookstore in the next block. She spent nearly twenty minutes in there, emerging with the complacent conviction that her own was better. Next door to it was the seafood restaurant. With the sensation that she was doing something momentous, Caroline pushed open the door.

It was pleasantly, if unoriginally, decorated with aquaria and fishnets and buoys, the blue and white checked tablecloths crisp and clean, the music unobtrusive. Caroline asked for a table by the window, where the light would give her an excuse to keep on her dark glasses, and sat down facing the door. For all that she was quite safe in here, she did not want Sean Reilly creeping up behind her. She ordered a Manhattan, and began leisurely perusing the room.

A group of young people came in, filling a table for eight, and ordering, predictably enough, large quantities of french fries, milk shakes, onion rings, and hot dogs. A very matronly woman with a shelf-like bosom and the kind of hat Caroline's grandmother used to wear sat down a couple of tables away and ordered tea and muffins. And then the black-haired man walked in.

Caroline buried her face in the menu, the words dancing in front of her eyes. All of a sudden she wished she hadn't embarked on this adventure. Indoors Sean Reilly was much larger than she had thought, his brow marked by a formidable frown. *Tough and dangerous*, Gabrielle had called him. . . .

She swallowed hard. All she had to do was keep her head, delay him perhaps another hour, and then tell him who she really was. He would be angry, of course, but that was beside the point; by then Gabrielle would be long gone.

The waitress, a pretty blonde girl who had the look of a college student, arrived with her drink. 'Are you ready to order, ma'am?'

'Why, Gabrielle! What a pleasant surprise . . . do you mind if I join you?'

Caroline looked up, allowing herself a moment or two of puzzled silence before saying slowly, 'It's Sean, isn't it? Sean Reilly?'

'Martin's brother.'

'Of course——'

'Surely you haven't forgotten him, even if you have forgotten me?'

There was a note in his voice that caused a frisson to travel up and down her spine; however, she had never been one to refuse a challenge. 'I haven't forgotten either of you. Please, do sit down, Sean.'

'Can I get you something from the bar, sir?'

'Scotch on the rocks, please.' He gave the waitress a quick smile which had the effect of reducing the girl to a dumbstruck silence, Caroline saw impatiently. She herself was quite ready to agree with Gabrielle's description of him, right down to the clouded grey eyes; he was devastatingly attractive, his smile with a vitality and warmth that must make women fall for him in droves. But not this woman, she thought tartly. *She* knew what he was really like underneath that undeniable charm and—Gabrielle was right again—that smouldering masculinity.

'Have you ordered?' he asked prosaically.

'No, I was about to. Scallops, french fries and a tossed salad, please, with a glass of milk.'

Sean Reilly had swiftly scanned the menu. 'I'll have the same, but coffee instead of milk. . . . So, Gabrielle, what brings you to these parts?'

The first move in the game they were both playing, a double game with very different ends. 'Believe it or not, I'm here on holiday,' she responded lightly. 'Enjoying the sun and the beaches. And yourself?'

'Very much the same. A friend of mine has a summer place on Deep River, so I'm staying there for a few days. This is quite a coincidence.'

The frisson touched her spine again, for although his mouth was smiling, the grey eyes were as cold as a winter sky. 'I'm staying at the Newport Inn,' she remarked.

'It looks a bit like a gingerbread house, doesn't it?' The waitress brought his drink, and he raised his glass, his eyes trained on Caroline's face. 'What would be an appropriate toast, Gabrielle? Should we drink to Martin?'

'I scarcely think that would be appropriate.'

'Perhaps you're right. You should know, after all. How about to our summer holidays, will that do?'

She sipped from her glass, feeling the rye whisky bite her palate. 'I certainly prefer that.'

'I do wish you'd take off those glasses,' he said irritably, 'I hate talking to someone who's hiding behind a pair of coloured lenses.'

She would have preferred not to; not this soon. But the whisky had warmed her throat and the adrenalin was coursing through her veins, and momentarily Gabrielle was forgotten: the conflict was between her, Caroline, and this hard-eyed stranger. She reached up and took off the glasses, putting them on the table beside her plate and then looking him full in the face, her chin raised, her expression disdainful.

'You're even more beautiful than I remember.' Her lashes flickered as he frowned. 'And I certainly don't remember your eyes being that dark a blue,' he added slowly.

'You only met me the one time. And as I recall, you disliked me instantly. I should imagine the exact colour of my eyes was not one of your chief concerns.'

'Would you now? It could be that you're quite wrong. . . .'

He had the knack of throwing her off balance. 'Admit it, Sean,' she said boldly. 'You never gave me a chance. You were prejudiced against me right from the start.'

'As it turns out I've been proved right, haven't I?' he said silkily, taking a deep draught of his drink. 'To Martin's cost. Certainly not to yours.'

She glowered at him. 'See what I mean? You're not even trying to see it from my point of view.'

He sat back. 'Oh? Well, we have lots of time, Gabrielle. Why don't you try explaining it from your point of view? Here I am—a captive audience.'

Her cheeks were flushed with temper, her eyes wide-held. 'I find it hard to believe that you're really Martin's brother. I can't imagine two men being any more different. He's kind and gentle, while you—you're the most arrogant and critical man I've ever met!'

'You devastate me.'

Caroline tossed back a good quarter of her drink and replaced the glass with a snap as the waitress brought them a wicker basketful of fresh homemade rolls. Picking one out of the basket, Caroline broke it and buttered it, the ordinary little actions giving her the time to cool down. Losing her temper had not impressed him in the slightest, she realised belatedly. Perhaps other tactics would be more effective . . . besides which, there was something she really did want to say to him. Raising her eyes to his face, she said more calmly, 'It would seem you have something of the same effect on me as I have on you.'

'The sparks do fly, don't they?'

'Sean, I'm sorry about what happened to Martin, more sorry than I can say . . . I loved him, after all.' She played with her knife, one small part of her brain recognising that she very much disliked red nail polish. 'But it would never have worked out for us, and I'm sure I did the right thing. I'm only sorry it turned out the way it did.'

'Sorry is not a particularly adequate word under the circumstances.' His mouth was a thin line, his face hard and unforgiving.

'I see. I suppose it's natural that you should see it that way.'

'Natural enough. How do you think I feel when I go and visit him, and see him locked up in that place?'

He was holding a savage anger in control, but only just. She whispered, 'How is he?'

'Your concern is very touching, Gabrielle. But I'm sure you'll understand if I say I'd prefer not to answer that question. You've forfeited the right to any kind of involvement with Martin, even to the extent of me discussing him with you.'

'Everything's black and white to you, isn't it? I'm black as pitch, while you and Martin are lily-white. The bad guys and the good guys. I would have thought you were old enough to know that life is never that simple, Sean. That there are a million shades of grey in between the absolutes of good and evil.'

'With anyone else a philosophical discussion the nature of evil would be very interesting, but not with you. Drop it, Gabrielle. You'll never convince me in a hundred years that you're anything but a selfish, gold-digging little bitch who used my brother when it was convenient for you and then dropped him the moment he became a liability.' He broke off. 'Here comes our food. For God's sake, let's leave the subject of Martin and endeavour to enjoy our meal like a couple of civilised human beings.'

So he had lost his temper, too ... and strangely Caroline was visited by the conviction that he had not intended to, that he was angry with himself for doing so. She sat in silence as their plates were put in front of them, accompanied by wooden bowls of salad and a flask of dressing.

'Will that be all, sir?' the waitress piped, giving Sean another besotted look.

'A carafe of the house wine, please. White.' As the girl left, he muttered, 'It'll no doubt be awful, but I need it. And when it comes, we'll drink to a truce. All right?'

Caroline had had time to recover. 'All right,' she echoed, adding with a glimmer of humour, 'What shall we discuss—the weather?'

'Politics, religion, the best-seller list. What movies have you seen lately, and did you go south last winter?'

'Movies,' she replied promptly. 'I'm an addict. I have this secret yen to be Katharine Hepburn or Liv Ullmann, and I know I haven't got a hope. Or else,' she added wistfully, 'to play opposite Paul Newman. He's so gorgeous, isn't he?'

It was the first time Sean's smile had reached his eyes. It made him look younger and more carefree, so that as they discussed Hollywood's latest offerings and the state of the film industry in Canada, Caroline found herself wondering how old he was. Early thirties? It was hard to tell. While there was a fan of tiny lines at the corner of each eye, and a touch of grey in the thick, silky hair, he was very tanned, the deep tan of a youthful, active man who spends a great deal of time outdoors. He was wearing an open-necked shirt, the sleeves rolled up to the elbows. Not a particularly close-fitting shirt, indeed a very ordinary shirt. Yet there was no disguising the smooth play of muscles under the cotton fabric, nor the fact that he was in superb physical condition. Not a man to tangle with, she decided ruefully, trying to ignore something else that the clothes could not hide: sexy, Gabrielle had called him, and Gabrielle had been right.

The talk moved to other subjects, Caroline forgetting

that she was Gabrielle from Quebec and rather being herself, not afraid to express her opinions yet always ready to listen to—and argue with—the other point of view. Richard had not approved of this side of her character; his word on world politics and economics was the final word as far as he was concerned. So now it was a pleasure for Caroline to indulge in a two-way exchange, and she felt a dawning respect for Sean's intelligence, tolerance, and wit. It was a pity, she found herself thinking, that he was so judgmental and unbalanced on the subject of Martin; otherwise, she might have begun to like him a great deal, and to wish she had met him in less inauspicious circumstances.

She could not be blind to the fact that he seemed to be enjoying himself too, and she was pleased that it was so. By the time they had demolished lemon meringue pie and drunk their coffee, there was an easy companionship between them. They wrangled amicably over the bill, Caroline insisting on paying her share, and then, together, they left the restaurant.

It was cooler now, the sun sinking to the horizon and bathing the nearly deserted street in a warm, golden light that softened the outlines of the buildings and cast deep shadows on the sidewalk. 'Now that would be an intriguing light for a scene in a movie, wouldn't it?' Sean remarked.

She laughed. 'I have difficulty picturing Paul Newman in front of the Baptist church, though!'

He put a hand casually under her elbow. It was the first time he had touched her; she was faintly dismayed to find that she liked it. Maybe it was time to tell him she was not Gabrielle . . . maybe then they could spend the evening together as Caroline and Sean, without the shadow of Martin between them. But before she could decide how to begin, he said, 'Why don't I drive you back to the hotel? I'm sure this is a very safe place, but I'm still enough of a city person to dislike seeing a woman walking alone at dusk.'

That he should concern himself for her safety pleased her; she would tell him the truth about herself in the car. She was sure he would be angry with her for the deception, but equally she was confident that once he got over his anger he would be pleased to find she was not Gabrielle, whom he disliked so thoroughly, but somebody else altogether, a girl with whom he had enjoyed companionship and laughter. As they walked along past the shops where she had so carefully wasted time before their meal, she stole a glance at her watch, seeing that over two hours had passed. So she had more than fulfilled her bargain with Gabrielle.

The red sports car, she saw with a lift of her eyebrows, was a Porsche. Gabrielle had been proved right again, for she had said there was money in the family. Caroline waited while Sean unlocked the door, then slid into the bucket seat, which was upholstered in pale cream leather. The car's interior was exquisitely finished and spankingly clean; it even smelled expensive. It was a pity it was such a short distance to the hotel, since she had never driven in a Porsche before.

Sean got in beside her, putting the keys in the ignition, starting the car, and smoothly pulling out into the street, all without a word. Because they were heading in the opposite direction to the hotel, Caroline expected him to take the first side street in order to turn around. But he did not. They passed the shops and the restaurant, a gas station and a neat row of bungalows, and he shifted gears as the car gathered speed. The houses were more widely spaced now, fields and trees replacing the buildings of the town.

Caroline said uncertainly, realising she was stating the obvious but not knowing what else to say, 'We're going the wrong way.'

Sean did not answer. She glanced over at him. His profile was towards her with its strong, determined chin and set mouth; he was concentrating completely on his driving, ignoring her as if she did not exist. She repeated more strongly, 'Sean, we're going the wrong way.'

'No, we're not.' Flicking on his signal light and checking his mirrors, he passed a lumbering oil truck.

'The hotel is the other way.'

'But we're not going to the hotel.'

Caroline pushed back a surge of pure panic, not wanting to spoil her relaxed mood, not yet ready to admit she might have made a dreadful mistake by so thoughtlessly getting into his car. 'So what is this? A pleasant evening drive? Sean, I love your car, and I enjoyed talking to you in the restaurant but I'd really like to go back now, please.'

He whipped past a station wagon packed full of children and a very large dog. 'No dice.'

She had not become a downhill ski champion without having a fair degree of nerve. 'So where are we going?' she said coolly.

He shot her an inimical look. 'You'll see.'

'Really, you're behaving like the hero in a television serial—they're always tearing off into the sunset in red sports cars,' she snapped.

'Then why don't you try behaving like the heroine, and sit there in an admiring silence?' he retorted sarcastically.

'Because I certainly do not feel one bit of admiration for what you're doing!'

'Come on, Gabrielle, grow up. You surely didn't think it was coincidence that we met today?'

He was having me followed . . . I'm frightened of him, Gabrielle had said. Swiftly Caroline made her decision. 'Look,' she said calmly, 'it's time for a bit of plain speaking——'

'Good. I thought you'd come to that. Whatever your faults, and you have many of them, you were never a stupid woman.'

'You have the wrong woman, Sean. I'm not Gabrielle Cartier.'

'Of course not, you're Katharine Hepburn.'

She held tightly to her temper. 'My name is Caroline Travers. I own and operate a bookstore in Halifax. I have never seen you before today, and I have never met your brother.'

He quirked an eyebrow. 'Well, this is an interesting new angle. Do tell.'

Her palm itched to slap that sardonic look from his face. 'I met Gabrielle quite by chance this afternoon in the hotel. As you see, we look quite a bit alike——'

'Indistinguishable, I would say.'

'You mentioned yourself that my eyes were darker.'

'We were in a nightclub when I met you—remember? And you were wearing rather a lot of make-up, as I recall.'

Gabrielle had not mentioned the nightclub. Refusing to be discouraged, Caroline picked up the thread of her story. 'We were so struck with the resemblance that we went to my room to talk. She told me about Martin and how she'd seen you today. She was frightened of you, she said you were out for revenge——'

'You're right, I am.'

Again that flick of fear across her nerve endings. 'She asked me to change clothes, and to go outside, pretending to be her. You'd follow me, she said, and that would allow her to disappear. So that's what we did. And as you see, it worked. But the game's over now, and I'd like to go back to the hotel.'

His answer was to increase speed. Speed *per se* had never frightened Caroline, indeed it had always exhilarated her, and even now situated as she was, she found time to admire his skill behind the wheel. 'Have you ever been a racing driver?' she heard herself ask.

'You know damn well I haven't been. We talked about it that night and I told you how I was a test driver for the Porsche company in Germany for a while. Come on, Gabrielle, stop acting the wide-eyed innocent.'

'I'm *not* Gabrielle!'

'Right. You're Caroline somebody-or-other from Halifax who just happens to look exactly like Gabrielle whom you just happened to meet on the very day I caught up with her. It won't work, you know.'

He had slowed to make a left turn, and for a wild moment she contemplated jumping out. As if he had read her mind, Sean added, steel-voiced, 'The door is locked. And the controls are on my side.'

Caroline folded her hands in her lap, trying very hard to think rather than succumb to the fear that was eating away at her composure. 'I can prove I'm Caroline Travers,' she said finally. 'I have my driver's licence and my credit cards in my wallet.'

'I'll look at them when we get there.'

'Get *where*?'

'Where we're going,' was the lazy reply. 'Stop fretting and enjoy the scenery.'

Caroline stared out of the window, not knowing what else to do, for the first time paying some attention to their surroundings. They were following the winding course of a deep, high-banked river, its currents surging in the dark waters. Although the cliffs were shadowed from the last rays of the sun, the trees on the bluffs were still gold-tipped, while the lights of scattered houses shone like tiny beacons on the far shore. The road was narrow, full of curves, sudden declines, and equally steep hills. She had no idea where they were, and mentally castigated herself for not bothering to look at the road sign when they had turned left.

The houses on this side of the river were few and far between, she saw with a sinking heart. But somehow she had to get to one of them and ask for help ... somehow. One thing was certain. She could do nothing while they were still moving. Sooner or later they would stop somewhere, and then she must try and make her escape.

They drove for perhaps another twenty minutes

before turning off on to a dirt track, narrower than its predecessor and shaded by tall trees that crowded right to the ditches. It was almost dark now, the beams of the headlights making it seem darker than it really was, and despite all her efforts to stay calm, Caroline could feel tension mounting in her body, tightening her chest and throat. There was something very sinister about their solitary journey through the woods; they had crossed over a small plank bridge with white-painted railings, but that had been the only sign of civilisation on the road, and all the horror stories she had ever read about murder and rape came crowding into her mind. She was physically very fit, but she was no match for Sean Reilly, she knew that without even putting it to the test. And running, since she had broken her leg in that last disastrous competition in Sarajevo, had not been her strong suit. So what was she to do?

The car bumped down a hill, where recent rain had carved runnels in the road, then climbed up the next slope. As they topped it, Caroline saw, shining through the trees, a single light. Sean said flatly. 'That's the house.'

The trees thinned and the track emerged on to a grassy field. The light shone from one corner of a sprawling grey-shingled house, its natural wood door and neat white trim looking ludicrously normal after the nightmares that had been tormenting Caroline's mind. A big black and tan Alsatian, its tail wagging a welcome, got up from the stone step and sauntered out to meet the car.

Sean turned off the motor. 'Before we get out, the dog's name is Baron. He's a trained guard dog. If you behave yourself, he won't bother you. But if you try and run away, he'll bring you back. So don't try, okay?'

Caroline said nothing. She stared down at her clasped hands as Sean got out of the car, went around the hood, and opened her door. Slowly she climbed out.

The air smelled sweetly of new-mown grass overlaid

with the rich, damp odour of the river. The leaves were rustling softly on the trees, while high above them the first stars had already pierced the blackness of the sky. But any illusion of peace or pastoral simplicity was shattered as Baron approached them. He was a beautiful dog, his coat shining with health, his golden eyes expressive of intelligence, his big head level with Sean's thigh. Sean said firmly, touching Caroline on the arm, 'Guard her, Baron. Guard.' Then he let his hand drop to his side, as if the brief contact had been repugnant to him. 'Let's go inside.'

Caroline held back, unable to totally disguise the quiver in her voice. 'Why are we here?'

'I would have thought it was obvious,' he said curtly. 'I'm going to keep you here until you agree to co-operate with me. I want Martin out of that place.'

Her mouth was dry. 'And what am I supposed to do? I know you think it's all my fault, but surely Martin has to bear some responsibility for himself.'

She could hear his hiss of indrawn breath. 'I wish to God you'd drop this pose of wide-eyed innocence, Gabrielle—you know damn well you planted the stuff on him before he went across the border. So he took the rap instead of you.'

The nightmare swirled around her again, for it seemed as though even words had lost their meaning. 'What stuff?' she said baldly. 'I don't know what you're talking about.'

For a moment she thought he was going to strike her and she flinched backwards. He spat an epithet at her and said roughly, 'Heroin, Gabrielle, heroin. Martin was caught at the U.S. border with ten ounces of heroin in his overnight bag—and you put it there. So now he's in prison, and there he'll stay until you confess. Which is why you're here. The only way you'll leave here is to go with me to the police and make a full confession that will exonerate Martin. Have you got that straight?'

She shrank back, for she had never heard such naked

fury in anyone's voice before or seen such loathing in a man's eyes. 'Martin's in a mental hospital,' she faltered. 'That's what Gabrielle told me. That he'd had a nervous breakdown after she broke off their engagement.'

'Martin's in the penitentiary. And you're going to get him out,' Sean snarled. 'I've had enough of this nonsense. Let's go inside,' Turning his back to her as if he could not stand the sight of her, he headed towards the house.

Caroline had less than a moment to make up her mind. The whole world had gone crazy and she was more frightened than she had ever been on the ski slopes, even in that split second when she had known she was going to collide with the fence. Her one urge was to run—run as she had never run in her life before. She only had Sean's word for it that Baron would chase her; the dog seemed totally uninterested in her as he padded at his master's heels. Pivoting, she began to race for the trees.

The ground was uneven and it was too dark to judge where to put her steps. With a strength born of desperation she tore across the grass, dimly hearing a man shout. Reaching the edge of the lawn, she plunged into grass that was knee-high. But the trees were nearer now and once she reached them she'd be out of sight ... and then she heard it. The swish of grass. The rhythmic thud of a pursuer fast catching up on her. A panting breath. And then a great weight caught her from behind, throwing her off balance so that she crashed to the ground. The breath knocked from her lungs, she lay still, her eyes squeezed shut, waiting with the calm of despair for the first tear of teeth.

Nothing happened. She heard Baron whimper, then heavy footsteps approached through the grass. Sean dropped on his knees beside her. Her shoulder was seized and she was pulled over on her back. The swear word he used this time made her blink; opening her eyes, she heard him demand, 'Are you hurt?'

'N-no.'

'I told you not to run away!'

Caroline had sustained far worse falls in her skiing days, and the sheer relief of not being torn limb from limb by the dog made her say furiously, 'What would you have done if you'd been me? I never did. think much of lambs going meekly to the slaughter.'

'I'm not going to murder you, for God's sake—what would be the point of that?'

'I have no idea,' she retorted with considerable asperity, struggling to sit up. 'I think you're crazy— clean out of your mind! You're the one who should be in a mental hospital, not Martin!'

He shook her, his voice rough with anger. 'Martin's in prison!'

Ignoring him, she swept on, 'So how am I supposed to anticipate what you're going to do?'

'From now on you'd better pay more attention.' With scant ceremony he put his arm around her to help her up, his face very close to hers. Her eyes had adjusted to the darkness now and in a flash of intuition she thought, *he hates this. He's not nearly as tough as he sounds.* And then another thought followed hard on its heels. *I like being held by him.*

But how could she? The man was mad. He'd virtually kidnapped her and now she was blushing like a seventeen-year-old because he'd put his arm around her.

She drew away from him, wincing as she discovered sore spots where she had hit the ground. Sean got to his feet, putting his hands under her elbows and pulling her upright. For a moment her bad leg refused to take her weight so that she fell against his chest. 'Damn!' she muttered fretfully.

'What's wrong?' he demanded, suspicion sharpening his voice.

Against her cheek she felt the heat of his skin through his shirt and a treacherous warmth curled itself around her heart. She fought it down. She was the crazy one, she thought ruefully. She'd never felt like this in her life before. So why did she have to pick on a man who was little better than a kidnapper?

Irritably he repeated, 'What's wrong?'

'Nothing. It's an old injury, it'll be all right in a minute.' Gingerly she tested her weight on the leg, and this time it held her.

Sean kept an arm around her all the way down to the house, for she was still limping. Baron walked placidly beside them, his pink tongue lolling from his jaws. As she waited for Sean to unlock the front door, Caroline couldn't help noticing the dog's curved white teeth, and she gave a reminiscent shudder. No more running away—that much she knew.

After the three of them had gone indoors, Sean pulled the door shut behind them, snapping on a couple of lights. In spite of all that had happened, Caroline gave a low murmur of delight. They were looking into the sitting room, its ceiling with hand-hewn pine beams, its hardwood floor covered with a subtly shaded Oriental rug; a comfortable, velvet-covered chesterfield set was arranged around the massive stone fireplace.

'Come up to the bathroom,' Sean said abruptly. 'You've got dirt on your face.'

On their way to the stairs she caught a glimpse of a cosy, Spanish-tiled kitchen hung with begonias and ivy. The ultra-modern bathroom, decorated in cool shades of ivory and Wedgwood blue, had wicker appurtenances. Caroline looked at herself in the mirror. Gabrielle's sleek hairstyle had become Caroline's ruffled one: her auburn hair had a tendency to curl that she could never quite subdue. There was indeed dirt on her cheek, not to mention grass stains on the elegant silk shirt.

Sean had been holding a facecloth under the hot tap.

He wrung it out and passed it to her in silence. She rubbed her face, feeling her heartbeat quiet down and some of her normal self-possession come back to her. 'Thank you,' she said politely. 'Now, if you wouldn't mind fetching my handbag from the car, we'll clear up this misunderstanding once and for all and then maybe you'll take me back to the hotel.'

'I'll certainly fetch your handbag. Why don't you go down to the kitchen and put the kettle on? Baron will go with you, by the way, so don't try anything.'

'I wouldn't think of it,' she responded dryly.

The kitchen was every bit as pleasant in its own way as the living room. Copper pots and bundles of herbs hung from the slanted ceiling, while flowering plants were clustered in the wide expanse of window that presumably faced south; Caroline had always had a terrible sense of direction. She filled the kettle, noticing also that the kitchen was very clean, and took milk out of the well-stocked refrigerator. And then she heard Sean coming back and unconsciously her nerves tightened.

He gave her the teal-blue leather bag without comment. She pulled out her wallet, and, not bothering to open it, passed it to him. He opened it, unsnapping the flap that protected her cards, and flipped through them. Then he said levelly. 'I really don't know why you're persisting in this charade, Gabrielle. You're wasting my time and yours.'

Her heart skipped a beat. 'Pass me the wallet,' she said in a clipped voice.

When he did so, the first thing she saw was the driver's licence. An out-of-province driver's licence, in the name of Gabrielle Cartier. The colour drained from her face. Her fingers shaking, she found an outdated credit card and an old library card, both in Gabrielle's name. Of her own licence, credit cards, and family photographs, there was no sign.

The room dipped and swayed. Gabrielle had lied to

her, she thought sickly. Her mind flew back to the meeting in the hotel room, and she saw instantly how it had been done. While she, Caroline, had been fixing her hair and nails in the bathroom, Gabrielle had cold-bloodedly exchanged the contents of their wallets. The address Gabrielle had given her in Vancouver was the same address on the driver's licence; Caroline would be willing to bet it was fictitious. She'd been made a fool of. On the basis of an astonishing physical likeness, she had trusted a complete stranger ... something her mother had warned her about years ago.

She said in a voice scarcely recognisable as her own, still staring down at the wallet, 'Martin really is in prison,' and it was more statement than question.

Sean did not bother answering. He made them each a cup of instant coffee, putting them on the drop-leaf table nestled in an alcove by the window. 'Do you want anything to eat?'

'No, thanks.' Her mind had gone completely blank. She could not think what to do next; she certainly had no idea how to convince Sean Reilly she was Caroline Travers, an innocent—and gullible—tourist. She sat down, resting her elbows on the table and leaning her head in her hands, utterly exhausted.

The silence stretched out. She could not even find the energy to drink the coffee, and finally Sean said, 'You'd better go to bed. I'll show you your room.'

Obediently she followed him up the stairs again, Baron's claws scraping on the bare wood. Her room was halfway down the hallway, a spacious room facing away from the river, with a fourposter bed, hooked rugs on the floor and a massive cherrywood bureau. A feminine, dainty room with its frilled tester and lacy curtains; at any other time she would have been delighted to have slept in it. She said bluntly, 'Where do you sleep?'

'Across the hall.' He smiled unpleasantly. 'Don't worry, rape isn't my speciality. I prefer to at least like the woman I sleep with. Incidentally, there are no locks in any of the doors upstairs, but Baron will be out in the hall.'

Caroline said expressionlessly, only wanting him to be gone so she could collapse on to the bed and sleep, 'Goodnight.'

'Goodnight, Gabrielle. I'd suggest you do some hard thinking between now and tomorrow morning. I'm sure you've escaped from some tight spots before—but this one you're not getting out of!'

She could think of nothing to say. She waited until he had gone out, closing the door with exaggerated care behind him, then looked around the room. If this were a movie, there'd be a chair of just the right size to fit under the door handle. However, apart from the bed, the only other piece of furniture was the bureau, and she was quite sure she could not shift that.

There was no sound from the hallway, and the bed with its old-fashioned quilt and spotless print sheets was beckoning to her far more imperatively than her residual fears of being bothered by Sean Reilly. She took off all her clothes except for her lace-edged underwear and slid between the sheets. Her last thought before she fell asleep was what a fool she had been. What an unutterable, stupid fool. . . .

CHAPTER THREE

THE mournful cry of a gull soaring over the house woke Caroline in the morning. For a moment she lay still, staring up at the ruffled canopy over her head, wondering where she was and what she was doing in this strange bed. Then, outside her door, she heard a rattle of claws, a thud, and a heavy sigh ... Baron, shifting position. She was in Sean Reilly's house, virtually a prisoner.

No use in trying to go back to sleep. She got up, dressing in the new jeans and the crumpled silk shirt, then peering out of the window at an overcast, grey morning, the tree-tops swaying in the wind, the dark-edged clouds heavy with rain. Her view was necessarily limited by the angle of the window; there was nothing to see but grass, trees, and sky. No houses. No people. Her vague idea of signalling for help died stillborn.

Her lips set in a mutinous line, she opened the door. Baron raised his beautiful head from his paws, regarding her gravely. As she tried to step over him, he growled, a low warning rumble in his throat. Caroline stopped dead, her nostrils flaring with temper. This was ridiculous! What was she supposed to do, stay in her room all day?

The door across from hers swung open. Baron's tail hit the floor in a series of thumps as Sean emerged from his bedroom. He was wearing a pair of lean-fitting cords and nothing else. Dark hair curled on his chest, narrowing to a V at his navel; beneath the deeply tanned skin muscle and bone showed an elegant symmetry, fluid in movement, powerful in repose. Tall and well-built as he was, he was not at all clumsy; she had already noticed the economy and grace of his movements.

There were only a couple of feet—and the dog—between them. Caroline moved back a step, knowing she had been staring at him, horrified by the sensation flooding her body. A well-remembered sensation that had been her companion for years; a mingling of terror and excitement as she waited at the gate for the bell to ring so she could begin her headlong descent of the slope. She had experienced it time and again on the ski slope. In a far more intellectual way, she had also felt it in the early, challenging days of the bookstore when she had had no idea whether the venture would win or lose. But she had never felt it with a man before. She had certainly never felt it with Richard, she recognised dazedly.

'Come off it, Gabrielle,' Sean said irritably. 'You've seen plenty of men with considerably less on than this.'

'I'm not Gabrielle, I'm Caroline,' she answered automatically. 'Am I to be allowed to go to the bathroom and then have some breakfast?'

His mouth tightened. 'Of course you are. Baron will stay up here with you. I'll go and put the coffee on. Come down when you're ready.' To the dog, 'Guard, Baron.'

Twenty minutes later Caroline was feeling much better after a shower and shampoo, although she hated putting on the same stained blouse again. When she went into the kitchen Sean said briefly, 'You can borrow a clean shirt of mine for now if you want to. When I go into town this morning, I'll pick up a few clothes for you.'

She was not the exhausted, frightened girl she had been the night before. Helping herself to coffee without being asked, she said calmly, 'Look, don't you think this has gone far enough? I'm not Gabrielle Cartier. Believe me, I wish I'd never laid eyes on her and I'll never again offer to fill in for someone else . . . I've learned my lesson in that respect. My name is Caroline Travers, I'm a perfectly respectable owner of a bookstore in Halifax, and you simply can't keep me here like this. Apart from anything else, it's highly illegal.'

He gave her an ironic smile as he broke two eggs into the frying pan on the stove. 'Butter the toast for me, will you? You're a fine one to talk about legalities, Gabrielle. The business you're in isn't exactly legal—quite apart from its lack of moral scruple.'

'And what business am I supposed to be in?'

'Drug-dealing,' he said mildly. 'You're one of the middle-men—or I suppose I should say middle-persons, shouldn't I, in these days of Women's Lib? Nowhere near the top of the hierarchy, but not at the bottom either. A thoroughly despicable racket—although a fairly lucrative one, I should imagine.' He put two plates of bacon and eggs on the table and pulled out his chair. 'There's juice in the pitcher. That's how I found you, of course. Martin had told me two or three of the places you'd visited together, and I'd figured they were pick-up points. I tried the others with no luck, and this was the last. You should have been more careful.'

Feeling as though they were playing an intricate game of chess that under its surface politeness concealed a seething mass of emotion, Caroline said, 'When you're in town, go to the hotel. There's a room booked in the name of Caroline Travers. And my suitcase and bicycle are still there. Maybe that will convince you.'

He put jam on his toast. 'You'd better make up a list of what you'll need, along with the sizes.'

'You haven't listened to a word I've said!'

'You're a con artist, Gabrielle. Martin thought the sun rose and set with you, and he's not lacking in intelligence. You'll be touched to know that he still doesn't believe you had anything to do with the heroin that was planted in his bag. He refused to give the police your name when he was arrested, and he's never revealed it to them since then. He only told me after I kept on and on at him about everything he'd done and everyone he'd been with before the border crossing.'

'I bet you kept on and on at him,' she said nastily. 'The Spanish Inquisition would have nothing on you.'

As if she hadn't spoken, Sean continued, 'He'd be horrified if he knew what I was doing now.'

'I'm glad one of you shows some sensibility.' She began to eat, although her appetite had quite vanished. Oddly she would have felt better if Sean had sounded angry. But he was so matter-of-fact, so obdurate, that any other arguments she could think of seemed useless. As she finished the last of her coffee, she said, 'I don't have much money, I was going to go to the bank today. If you just buy me a T-shirt and some underwear, that'll do.'

'That won't be enough.'

'Well, I'm certainly not having you pay for my clothes!' she retorted, her eyes blazing.

A pecular expression crossed his face. 'As I recall, you were always only too ready to have someone else— anyone else—pick up the tab for you.'

She glared at him. 'I don't give a damn what Gabrielle was like. *I* don't want you paying for my clothes.'

He said smoothly, 'I'm beginning to understand why Martin was so taken in by you. If the drug market ever declines, you could always take up acting. You might even give Katharine Hepburn a run for her money.'

'Oh, you're insufferable!' she seethed, shoving back her chair and stalking over to the window to gaze sightlessly out over the river.

Sean's voice altered. 'You're limping.'

'My leg's sore this morning,' she said shortly.

'What happened to it?'

'I broke it skiing.' She braced herself for further

questions, for even after all this time she still disliked talking about the fall that had ended her skiing career.

But all he said was, 'I see. Let's clear up the dishes, and then I'll get going.'

Obscurely grateful for what could only be sensitivity, she helped him tidy the kitchen. It suddenly struck her how very strange this was: she, Caroline, involved in the little domestic tasks that married couples take for granted with a man who was virtually a stranger to her, and her avowed enemy. He had beautiful hands, she thought irrelevantly, as he passed her the dishtowel. His nails were well kept, the fingers long and lean, supple yet strong. Had she met him in any other circumstances, she would have found him powerfully attractive.

Hypocrite, her brain whispered to her. *You find him much too attractive as it is.*

Nonsense, she denied stoutly. *So he's got a sexy body . . . so what?*

Admit it, now—you'd like to run your hands up his chest and around his neck and kiss him . . . wouldn't you?

'What are you staring at me for?'

She blushed scarlet, almost dropping the cup she had been rubbing dry for far longer than was necessary. 'I——'

'I'm also beginning to understand why Martin wanted to marry you—you're the most beautiful woman I've ever seen.'

She shrank back before the look in his eyes. 'Don't——'

'Don't worry, I won't. Because underneath that lovely exterior is a shoddy little soul, Gabrielle . . . hard to believe, but true, nevertheless.' He turned away. 'I'm going into town, I'll be back in a couple of hours. The telephone's disconnected, and don't try to go outside, Baron won't let you.'

Five minutes later she heard the car engine start up and then diminish into the distance. She wandered into the living room, Baron padding along behind her, and

sat down on the cushions in the windowseat. The river
was a sullen grey serpent slithering between the banks;
even as she watched, the first drops of rain hit the
windowpane, driven by the wind. It was a cheerless
prospect, even a threatening one, and she should have
felt frightened and lonely. But strangely enough she did
not. Again she was visited by the strong sensation of
being perched on the brink of the hill, of excitement
and the thrill of victory being cupped in her palm.

She had never met a man remotely like Sean Reilly
before. She found she could recall every detail of his
torso, from the broad shoulders and straight back to
the hollowed collarbones and narrow waist, and
something stirred to life deep within her. She had not
felt at all like this with Richard. Why should she feel it
with Sean Reilly, who despised her? It was an
unanswerable question.

By rooting around Caroline found newspaper,
kindling, and logs, and lit a fire in the fireplace. From
the eclectic collection of records in the long cabinet
under the window she selected Verdi's *Aida*, for it
seemed the right kind of day to listen to that tormented
love story. Lying back on the chesterfield, she let the
music flow over her.

It was during the almost unbearably poignant third
act that Sean returned. It was raining hard now, pellets
of water rattling against the window like machinegun
fire, and when he came into the room, Caroline saw his
hair was soaked, his trench coat with dark patches on
the shoulders. The last tragic duet soared to the
heavens; in silence they both listened as the opera drew
to its inevitable close.

'Beautiful music,' Caroline said softly. 'The more I
hear it, the more affecting it seems.'

For a moment she thought he was going to reply in
kind. Then his face hardened. 'There was a Caroline
Travers at the hotel. But she checked out yesterday
afternoon taking her suitcase and her bicycle with her—

after you left for your walk. So you're not Caroline Travers. Q.E.D.'

She had been more or less expecting this, for she had checked her handbag after breakfast and found the room key and the key to the bicycle padlock both gone, another evidence of Gabrielle's duplicity.

'Didn't you ask what she looked like?'

'Why would I bother doing that? I know who you are.'

He looked so arrogant, so sure of himself. 'Have you never been wrong before?'

'Indeed yes—several times. But this isn't one of them.' He tossed a couple of big bags at her feet. 'Here are your clothes.'

It would have made a very effective gesture to have spurned them scornfully with her toe. Instead Caroline allowed curiosity to get the better of her and opened them, unaware that her expression was a little like that of a child opening an unexpected present. The T-shirt she had requested was a very pale yellow with a scooped neckline; the underwear was as pretty as she could have wished. She found herself blushing as she thought of him selecting the skimpy bikini panties and the lace-edged bra. But there was more. Socks, a pair of canvas sneakers, a shirt, some toilet articles, and, last of all, a full-length nightgown. She held it up. It was of navy blue nylon, severely cut, its bodice held by two tiny straps. Instinctively she knew it would look gorgeous on her.

She shoved it back in the bag. 'I'll keep the T-shirt, the underwear, and the toothbrush. The rest will have to go back—I don't have enough money.'

'You need something to sleep in.'

Refusing to look at him, her cheeks pink, she answered, 'You let me worry about that.'

'Really, Gabrielle, I would have wagered a bet you were long past the blushing stage.'

'Don't call me that!'

He seemed to lose interest. 'I'm going to have a shower. You might as well use the clothes, I'm certainly not taking them back.'

'I don't want to wear clothes you've paid for!'

'For heaven's sake,' he said in exasperation. 'What's the difference?'

'It may not matter to you. It does to me.'

'You've certainly developed some peculiar scruples since I first met you. Is that due to Martin's influence?'

Short of reiterating *My name is Caroline Travers*, rather like a robot, she had no answer for him. Fortunately he did not wait for one, but left the room. Baron thudded back down on the rug in front of the fire, his amber eyes closing. Caroline was not fooled. One move for the front door and the dog would spring to his feet, she was sure.

Lunch was a very silent affair, for Sean looked in a foul mood and Caroline could think of nothing to say that would not revive the conflict of Gabrielle versus Caroline. After they had cleaned up, she headed for the living room again, with the comfort of its log fire and its music. But as she was crossing the hallway Sean stopped her with a hand on her arm.

She tried to pull free, saying over her shoulder, 'Let go!'

His answer was to tighten his hold. She swung around to face him, finding herself only inches away from him; she could see the strongly etched nose, the unsmiling grey eyes and taut line of mouth, and was suddenly afraid. But she was not going to let him see that. 'What do you want?' she demanded, her chin tilted at a defiant angle.

'You had a very pleasant morning while I was out. But the object of this exercise is not to give you a holiday. I want something from you and I intend to get it. A signed confession, Gabrielle, and the assurance that you'll repeat the whole thing to the police.'

His fingers were like steel hooks digging into the soft

flesh of her arm. Her voice absolutely steady, even though inwardly she was quailing, she said, 'So what are you going to do? Bring on the thumbscrews?'

For a moment there was unwilling admiration in his eyes. 'You've got guts, I'll give you that . . . regrettably, that kind of thing's not in my line. No, you'll go to your room and you'll stay there. When you produce a confession, you can come downstairs. It's that simple. I know I only met you once, Gabrielle, but I still know quite a bit about you—you'll hate staying up there hour after hour by yourself. No one to talk to. Nowhere to go.'

'What do I get—bread and water?' Caroline asked in a brittle voice.

'You'll get your meals. Better meals than Martin's getting. And a hell of a lot more comfort.'

There was a raw savagery underlying his words. 'Have you visited him?' she asked, knowing the answer before she spoke yet unable to prevent the question.

'Of course I have . . . You even had it timed right, didn't you? You must have known from Martin that I was away on a cruise and wouldn't be back for four months when you made the border crossing. Clever of you. With me out of the way, Martin didn't have a chance. He's too kind and gentle, not a fighter like me—if I'd been around he wouldn't have gone to jail. You would have.'

His voice had been rising while he spoke; she had never seen such loathing in a man's face before. But there was pain under the loathing, she knew: the pain of a man of action who has to stand by and watch someone else suffer. It did not take much discernment to see that he loved his younger brother, and she was shaken by a sudden wave of compassion for him. No wonder he hated Gabrielle!

'How is he?' she asked in a small voice.

'He's surviving, but not much more. He's not made for that environment, he's not tough enough. And he's always had a tendency to claustrophobia—you must have known that. I don't suppose you gave it a second thought, did you?'

'You're hurting my arm!'

With a muffled expletive he dropped his hand to his side. 'Go on upstairs,' he ordered, 'Baron, guard.'

Caroline made one last attempt. Her dark eyes steady on his face, she said quietly, 'Sean, I swear by all that I hold dear that I am not Gabrielle Cartier. Every hour that you keep me here is undermining your chances of ever finding her again. She's a clever, unscrupulous woman, you know that better than I.' She risked putting her hand on his arm, feeling the warmth of his skin course through her fingers, alive and very real. 'You'll never free Martin if you persist in keeping me here. Because I can't confess to something I didn't do.'

'You know what's so horrible about all this,' he answered in an almost conversational tone of voice. 'I'm standing here listening to you, and I know you for what you are, and yet you have the voice of an angel and a beauty that nearly drives me crazy.' His lip curled in self-disgust. 'Go upstairs. I don't want to be in the same room with you.'

She had tried and she had failed. She turned away from him and went up the narrow staircase, Baron patiently following her. It was almost a relief to be alone with only the drumming of the rain on the roof for company. Feeling very tired, wishing she could banish from her mind the vision of a bearded young man confined to a prison cell, pacing up and down, up and down to keep the walls at bay, she took off her sandals—Gabrielle's sandals—and lay down on the bed, pulling the quilt up over her. She hated confined spaces herself, and always used stairs rather than elevators. How would she feel locked up in prison? Particularly for a crime she had not committed ... she'd hate it. She knew she would.

CHAPTER FOUR

CAROLINE awoke the next morning with a plan hovering in her brain. Sitting up in bed, resting her chin on her palm, she indulged in some concentrated thought. So far Gabrielle had succeeded in duping Martin, Sean, and herself, as a result of which Martin was in prison and Sean had become a kidnapper with her, Caroline, as his victim. How she must be laughing, that sleek, sophisticated French girl; Caroline, so trusting and naïve, had indeed been like a gift from heaven for her. But what could be done about it?

Certainly by staying here meekly as Sean's captive, nothing would be accomplished, for Caroline had spoken the literal truth when she had said to Sean that with every hour that passed the task of locating Gabrielle would become more and more of an impossibility. Gabrielle was probably already holed up at an unknown address with a new identity, she thought gloomily, grimacing to herself, for just as she had hated being defeated on the ski slopes, so she now thoroughly disliked the idea of Gabrielle getting the better of her. Not to mention the ever-present image of poor Martin behind bars for a crime he had not committed.

So she had to get out of here and somehow convince Sean she was not Gabrielle. But how to escape? Running away was out of the question, and she was quite sure Sean would not leave his car keys lying around for her to pick up, even if she could evade Baron long enough to reach the car. No, there had to be some other way.

Neatly the solution clicked into her brain: bring the rescuers to her, by a signal of some kind.

Half an hour later the plan was fully hatched.

Caroline had gone to the bathroom once Sean had called Baron off, had carefully locked the door, and under cover of the noise of the tap water had opened the window as wide as it would go. It was, as she had hoped, a dormer window with a sloping strip of roofing below it, wide enough to give her a foothold and enable her to get up on the roof proper. If she took a large white towel with her, she could signal from the very peak, and surely someone on the other side of the river would see her.

It was a plan with a fair certainty of success yet with just enough risk to appeal to her. If she disliked being fooled by Gabrielle, she also hated the thought of succumbing to Sean's dicta without putting up a bit of a fight. She was not afraid of him, she thought stoutly, shoving to the back of her mind the memory of the corrosive hatred in his eyes yesterday afternoon. Not really afraid. His plan of keeping her here until she confessed must seem very logical to him; that he had the wrong woman was scarcely his fault. Anyway, with a bit of luck she'd be able to get back into the bathroom without him even knowing she'd been on the roof. And if her signal had no effect the first time, she'd try again. Sooner or later someone would have to notice her.

Quickly she slid the window down again, grateful to the unknown owners of the house for having such well-fitting sashes. Giving her face a cursory wash and dabbing it quickly with the towel, she opened the door. 'Oh! Are you waiting to get in?' she said foolishly.

Sean was standing in the hallway, a breakfast tray in his hands, his face set and unsmiling. 'No. I was waiting to give you this.'

Sure that she must look the picture of guilt, she babbled, 'You don't need to bring my breakfast up—I could come down and get it.'

'I told you yesterday I didn't want you coming downstairs.'

So I'll go up on the roof instead, she thought recklessly. 'Then do allow me to relieve you of the tray so you don't have to spend a moment longer in my company than is necessary.'

'That's more like the real you,' he drawled. 'All this sweetness and light you've been projecting was getting a bit much.'

If earlier she had had any doubts about the wisdom of her plan, she certainly had none now. Glaring at him, she reached out for the tray, giving its contents a quick glance. 'Thank you,' she said ungraciously.

'I do assure you there's no arsenic in the coffee,' he replied blandly. 'Much as I might like to put it there.'

If only he wasn't so damnably attractive, Caroline thought crossly. A lock of hair had fallen across his forehead and she had the absurd urge to reach up and stroke it back, to feel for herself the warmth of his skin and the silky softness of his hair. As he relinquished the tray, their hands met. It was only a brief touch, undoubtedly accidental, but it jolted her nerves like a shock of electricity. His eyes were fathomless, giving nothing away. He hadn't felt anything. . . .

He said harshly, 'I've put a pen and paper in your room. You might do well to remember you're going to stay there until you write that confession.'

'I'm sure you'll remind me if I'm in danger of forgetting.'

'You might remember something else,' he grated. 'My patience isn't inexhaustible, Gabrielle. Every hour you delay is another hour on Martin's sentence. For your own good, it might be as well for you to give that some serious thought.' With one hand he very lightly encircled her throat. 'I won't tolerate an indefinite delay.'

The grey eyes were like stone, the mouth a thin, hard line, and Caroline's bravado evaporated. She *was* afraid of him. Particularly when he looked like that. His fingers had applied only minimal pressure, but he could not always be depended on to show such restraint. However, she stood her ground, a stubborn kind of pride refusing to allow her to cringe in front of him, or to beg him once again to believe in her true identity. She said flatly, 'My coffee's getting cold. Excuse me.' Her spine very straight, she walked into her room, put the tray on the bed and closed the door, seeing from the corner of her eye that he was still standing there. Watching her.

Her appetite had deserted her. Very briefly she rested her hand on her throat, hearing the lethal clarity of Sean's words echo in her head ... *my patience isn't inexhaustible. I won't tolerate an indefinite delay.* Thank heavens she had mapped out a plan of action, she thought, sitting on the bed and regarding the lukewarm coffee without enthusiasm. At least it would give her something to do. Anything would be preferable to sitting here all day and remembering that feather-light, deadly brush of fingertips on her flesh.

Mid-afternoon seemed the logical time for her roof-climbing expedition, for with luck at that time of day the residents across the river would be out in their gardens enjoying the sun. So at lunchtime, when once again Sean brought her a tray, she said with just the right degree of offhandedness. 'I want to wash my hair this afternoon. I suppose you won't let me dry it outdoors in the sun?'

He favoured her with an unpleasant smile. 'Right first time.'

The answer she had wanted. 'It would only take ten minutes,' she argued. 'What difference would it make?'

'That's ten minutes of your company I can do without.'

Although she had succeeded in her aim of establishing an alibi for herself in the bathroom without letting him know her real purpose, she felt a distinct hurt rather than a sense of accomplishment. It was Gabrielle he hated, not Caroline. But it was hard not to take it personally when he was looking at her as if she was some kind of slimy, loathsome creature he'd discovered under a rock and would like to crush with the heel of his shoe. She wanted him to like her; and there wasn't the slightest chance he would, she knew. She turned away, letting him see the sulky pout of her lips, and again she closed the door in his face.

Because Caroline was impatient by nature, the time seemed to crawl by until three o'clock, which for some reason was the time she had decided upon. Sean had stationed Baron at the foot of the stairs, so she crossed the hallway into the bathroom without any trouble, locking the door behind her. Turning on the tap, she slid the window open and removed the screen, managing to break only one fingernail in the process. Carefully leaning the screen against the bathtub, she took a big white towel from the cupboard, looping it around her neck, and turned off the water: she couldn't leave it running the whole time she was on the roof. Bending backwards, she eased herself out of the window feet first.

She was wearing the canvas sneakers Sean had bought for her, her rarely dormant sense of humour rather tickled by the idea of using them to effect her escape . . . it would serve him right. That the soles had a good grip was just as well, for the ledge was narrower than she had thought, and more steeply inclined. Clinging to the windowsill, trying not to notice the vertical drop to the ground, she inched her way along the ledge. On top of everything else she had to be as quiet as she could, for while Sean might not notice any strange sounds, Baron certainly would.

Finally she made it to the corner of the dormer. Clutching the edge, she began climbing up the roof. She had not realised quite how high it was, nor how sharply angled; it extended for at least ten feet above the peak of the dormer. She got down on all fours to give herself better balance, the sun-heated shingles rough on her bare knees . . . it was a lot easier going down a ski slope than up a roof, she soon decided.

By the time she reached the peak, Caroline was sweating. She sat down, bracing herself with her feet, the towel heavy on her neck, and for a moment lost all other concerns in the beauty of the scene in front of her. Like a goddess on her high perch, she could see across the deep, slow-moving river to the hills on the far shore, the houses dwarfed to neatly painted rectangles set in diminutive clearings, the trees a closely woven green blanket covering the slopes. It was further away than she had expected, and she felt the first qualm of doubt. The scheme that had seemed so certain of success in the bedroom seemed much less so from the angle of the roof.

Nevertheless, she removed the towel from around her neck and began to wave it up and down, holding it by the two corners. There was no sign of life across the river, no boats or swimmers in the water. Doggedly she kept on flapping the towel, up and down, up and down, feeling a bit of a fool. If anyone did see her, they'd probably have her committed along with Martin, for after all, what normal twenty-two-year-old woman would sit on top of a roof waving a towel? Former Ski Champion Takes to Roof Climbing. She could see the headlines now. Stubbornly she persisted, the sun hot on her shoulders, her arms already beginning to ache.

'What the *devil* are you doing?'

She jumped, her foot slipped on the shingles and she nearly lost her balance. Then she saw it was Sean standing on the ground below her with the faithful Baron at his heels, the two sets of eyes fastened on her antics. They looked a long way down. They also looked rather comical, foreshortened by distance, an audience of two. 'It was the devil made me do it!' she yelled, flashing Sean a wide smile, her teeth as white as the towel. An imp of mischief made her add, 'It's nice up here—you should try it sometime.'

'Gabrielle, get down from there!'

'I'm not Gabrielle!' She whirled the towel over her head. 'I'm a beautiful maiden in distress who's being held prisoner by a wicked baron.'

'I find it in me to pity the poor man,' Sean yelled back, his black hair gleaming in the sun. 'I'll count to ten and if you haven't started to climb down, I'm coming up to get you.'

'Oh good!' she shouted enthusiastically. 'Two of us on the roof should have twice the chance of attracting attention as one.'

'Get down, Gabrielle.'

'No!'

He disappeared from sight. Caroline waited, the smile still lingering on her lips. It would be interesting to see what Sean Reilly would do; already she recognised him as something of a kindred spirit. She had never felt like daring Richard to do anything ... because she had known he would disdain such childishness? It was certainly impossible to imagine Richard kidnapping anyone, particularly a woman. He would be too worried about his reputation to do that. Whereas Sean would do exactly as he pleased, regardless of reputation or consequences.

She was not left long in suspense regarding Sean's intentions. She heard a series of thuds, and realised he must be banging on the locked bathroom door; as it was not his own house, he would hardly play the movie hero and shatter the panels with his shoulder—a trick she had always secretly distrusted, certain it must be a lot more difficult to do than it appeared on the screen. Then she heard the sound of a window being raised. His bedroom window, also a dormer. He levered himself out the same way she had, although she couldn't help noticing, he was considerably more dexterous, or less afraid of the drop, then she had been.

He was perhaps twenty-five feet from her. The light breeze ruffled his hair as he straightened to his full height. 'Are you going to get down on your own, or do I have to come and get you?' he said.

She could not divine his mood from his tone of voice, but somehow she thought he was no longer the slightest bit amused by her escapade. 'What are you proposing to do?' she answered dulcetly. 'Pick me up and tuck me under your arm?'

'You really do see yourself as the movie heroine, don't you?' he flashed back. 'It's a twenty-foot drop to the ground, Gabrielle. In the movies they have inflated mattresses to catch you when you fall. But this is real. There's no mattress down there, only flagstones, and if you fall on those you'll break your neck. So stop being such a bloody fool and come down here—I'll help you in the window.'

'I bet you will. You'd be more likely to give me a good shove over the edge.'

'Don't tempt me, or I might,' he answered grimly. 'Get moving!'

Wondering just how far she could push him, Caroline put the back of her hand to her eyes and declaimed theatrically and with patent untruth, 'I can't get down—I'm afraid of heights.' Through the slits between her fingers she watched him, and saw a reluctant smile pull at his mouth. So he *was* a kindred spirit . . .

'Look, this is all very entertaining, but you're not Katharine Hepburn and I'm not Paul Newman, and I don't plan on spending the rest of the afternoon on a hot roof, tin or not. Edge along the pitch until you're level with me, and then crawl down backwards. 'I'll make sure you don't fall. As I believe I've said before, you're no good to me dead.'

She had very little choice. She couldn't get to the ground and even if she could Baron would be waiting for her, white fangs gaping. And she was getting sore from sitting so long on the hard roofing. She draped the towel around her neck again. Putting her palms and the soles of her feet flat to the roof, she began working her way down the slope by shifting her behind—not very dignified, but at least safe.

'I told you to come over this way first.'

'I don't need your help.'

She was almost level with the dormer by now. She risked a glance sideways and saw him moving swiftly towards her across the angle of the roof, leaning slightly inwards, every movement supple, fluid, and perfectly balanced. The cat burglar, she thought confusedly, wondering just what he did for a living. She'd be willing to bet he didn't sit at a desk. . . .

She stood up, gripping the sill with her right hand, her one desire to reach the window before he reached her.

Sean stopped dead. 'Be careful—you could fall,' he said urgently.

Suddenly it was no longer a game. Caroline turned to face him, her eyes glittering with rage. 'What do you care? You hate me.'

'Don't be an idiot, Gabrielle, this is no place to stage a row.'

His use of that hated name was the final straw. 'If I'm Gabrielle, maybe *you'd* better not get too close. I might try and push *you* over.'

There was no mistaking the menacing undertone in his voice. 'I don't advise you to try.'

He was crouching like a panther ready to spring, and an irrational panic gripped her by the throat. She forgot that she had precipitated the whole situation. All she knew was that she was afraid of him. Afraid of his lean, muscled body and his tamped-down hostility. What did she really know of him? Virtually nothing. And if looks could kill, she was good as teetering on the eaves over the sharp-edged flagstones.

She made a sudden lunge towards the bathroom window, not even thinking how this would throw all her weight on her bad leg, and then everything happened very fast. Her leg buckled under her so that she lost her balance and her shoulder crashed against the sharp corner of the sill. Her thin cry of pain was bitten off, her face a rictus of terror, for the eaves were coming up to meet her and the flagstones whirled in a crazy kaleidoscope in front of her eyes. She was going to fall ... as if it was happening to someone else, she felt pain as her knees scraped on the shingles and the rip of her fingernails in the wood. And then she was being seized and hauled back from the edge by sheer brute force, her body limp as a rag dool, her mind frozen with fear. Dimly she was aware of Sean pulling her through the open window and lowering her, not very gently, to the floor.

The tiles felt cold after the sun's heat; she was shaking like a leaf. Despising her own weakness, she tried to sit up, pushing herself up on her elbows, her hair falling forward over her face.

Sean grabbed her by the shoulders, and in automatic reaction her chin snapped up. Her lips were quivering, her eyes still glazed with the horror of that split second in time when she had thought she was going over the edge to crash on the stones below. He snarled, 'You little idiot! You nearly killed us both!'

She flinched back from the fury in the storm-grey eyes. But one of the prerequisites of a downhill ski racer is the ability to think and calculate at lightning speed, and even as she pulled away Caroline saw other things: a pallor under the bronzed skin, a tightness in his mouth, that told her more than words. He did not savour such physical confrontations, she thought slowly; he was a far cry from the macho hero who relished violence for the sake of violence. He had not enjoyed hauling her bodily across the window sill and dumping her on the floor, and part of the murderous rage she saw in him now was because she had thrust him into a role that was repugnant to him. It was only logical that she go one step further, acknowledging that it was all too likely he had disliked something else:

touching her, carrying her, holding her. What had he said her first night here? *I prefer to at least like the women I sleep with.*

'Didn't you hear me?' He shook her, although she could have sworn he had no idea he was doing it.

'Yes, I heard you.' She had recovered enough of her poise to add stubbornly, 'I would have been all right if you'd stayed away from me.'

'I thought you might fall,' he said shortly.

'Be honest, you don't give a damn about *me*. But if I'd fallen, it would have ruined your nice little kidnapping scheme, wouldn't it?'

'That's right. As I keep repeating to the point of boredom, you're no good to me dead.'

And no good to you alive. . . . 'I was in no danger of falling,' she said, suddenly weary of the whole thing. Without conceit, simply stating a fact, she went on, 'I've got very good balance. I'm an expert skier.'

'I believe you.' Again she saw reluctant admiration in his face. 'You've got one hell of a nerve, I'll tell you that. Did you and Martin ever go skiing?'

She sensed this was a trick question, that possibly Martin had never been near a pair of skis in his life. 'As I've never met him, it's highly unlikely,' she said lightly.

His eyes narrowed, his face so close to hers that she could see tiny flecks in the impenetrable grey of his irises. 'I don't know why I keep expecting you to tell the truth. Rather naïve of me, isn't it?'

'I am telling the truth.'

'You wouldn't know how.'

Her lashes flickered, and abruptly she became aware that her knees were stinging and her shoulder ached where she had crashed into the sill. *Why the hell do I care what he thinks of me?* she asked herself irritably, knowing even as she phrased the question that she was unable to answer it. 'Let go of me—I want to get up,' she said flatly.

If anything, his hands tightened their hold. 'If only

you weren't so goddamned beautiful,' he muttered. 'You could put a spell on a man with those big dark eyes of yours and that kissable mouth.'

She tensed, trying to pull free. 'Stop it!'

But he had lowered his head to hers. Paralysed by a mixture of emotions far more complicated than mere fear, Caroline felt the first touch of his lips against hers. His hands were still holding her with cruel strength; but there was nothing cruel or forceful in his kiss. His lips brushed over hers with exquisite gentleness, then stayed and warmed and deepened. For a moment her mouth was passive under his, shocked into immobility. But not for long. As if his mouth had brought the sun's heat to melt the winter snow, the tension eased from her body and her lips softened, moving shyly against his, delighting in an intimacy that in a strange way was totally new. She had been kissed before. Not even Richard was so cold-blooded not to have kissed her. But it had never been like this.

Very slowly Sean drew back. He must have seen the delicate flush on her cheekbones and the velvet softness of her eyes, and for a fleeting moment his own eyes were full of questions, as if the truth were to be found in the upturned face so close to his. Then they hardened. His hands dropped from her shoulders. 'If that's how you looked every time Martin kissed you, no wonder he was infatuated with you!'

His words ripped away the tenderness of a kiss that for Caroline had been a revelation. She stared at him so uncomprehendingly that he added harshly, 'You're over-acting, darling.'

She was not sure what was worse, to be called Gabrielle, or to be called *darling* with so much bitterness to a word that should be full of love. Struck dumb, she shifted her position, wincing with pain as her legs touched the floor. Glancing downwards, she saw without much interest that she had grazed both knees on the rooftop.

Sean had followed the direction of her gaze. 'How did you do that?' he rapped.

'When I fell. Which gives you the perfect opportunity to say it serves me right.'

He ignored her. 'I'd better bathe them for you. It looks as though you've picked up a couple of splinters as well.'

She could handle his anger more easily than this disinterested kindness. Perilously near tears, knowing that single devastating kiss had undermined her composure more than her near-fall, she said with assumed calm, 'I'd much rather do it myself, Sean, thank you.'

He shot her a quick glance, as if surprised by her reply. 'You've changed since I first met you—you were very much the clinging vine type in those days.'

'I haven't changed at all. I never was one of those clinging, helpless females—I can't stand them.'

A tiny pause. Then he answered leisurely, 'A good try, Gabrielle. But it won't wash, you know.'

'I'm tired of discussing it,' she snapped. 'Please will you leave so I can I get cleaned up.'

Not hurrying, he hooked the screen back in place, and partially closed the window. 'Can I assume you won't try the same trick twice?' he said, standing watching her with hands in his pockets.

'You certainly can!' she replied with such unexpected fervour that he laughed.

'Good. I never did see myself as Superman flying among the rooftops.'

Somehow he had made it easier for her to speak. Looking him straight in the eye, she said, 'It was foolish of me to go up there. It seemed a good idea at the time, and I didn't think about the danger. I—thank you for not letting me fall,' she finished in a rush, not very lucidly.

His hands were still in his pockets, but his stance was no longer relaxed. His black brows drawn together in a frown, he said, 'You've *got* to be Gabrielle . . . but you sure as hell aren't behaving much like her. I can't imagine she ever apologised for anything in her life.'

It was the first inkling of doubt about her identity that she had received from him. She held her breath, wondering if he would say anything more. He did, but not what she wanted to hear. Glowering at her, he muttered, 'You must find it very amusing that I should even consider this elaborate Caroline Travers story you've cooked up. It makes me almost as gullible as Martin, doesn't it?'

What could she say? *It's not a story, it's the truth. I don't behave like Gabrielle because I'm not Gabrielle. . . .* She might as well save her breath.

'There's a first aid kit in the medicine cabinet,' he said abruptly. 'I'll be downstairs if you need any help.' Turning on his heel, he went out of the room, closing the door behind him.

Caroline stayed where she was, conscious of a strong urge to put her head on her injured knees and cry her eyes out. She was not a girl who cried often or easily, and that she should want to now said rather more about her feelings towards Sean than she cared for. So he had kissed her and she had liked it—so what? Although like was too mild a word for the sweet ache of longing his lips had evoked, she was honest enough with herself to admit that. *He's just a man*, she thought fiercely, rubbing at her eyes, *a man like any other*.

Scrambling to her feet, she opened the medicine cabinet and began to clean the scrapes on her knees; the physical pain at least took her mind off Sean Reilly.

CHAPTER FIVE

FOUR days passed, days during which Caroline stayed in her room nearly the whole time, Sean bringing all her meals to her. She made a single trip to the bookshelves in the living room and loaded herself up with a varied assortment of books, several of which she had been meaning to read for months and had never got around to. Some were very light, pure entertainment: those she read at night to put herself to sleep. A tome on philosophy she could only tackle in the morning, while biographies of people as diverse as Golda Meir and Mozart she read through the long, quiet afternoons.

She was interested, amused, even excited by some of her reading; she also suffered from physical restlessness, loneliness, and boredom. But she was no longer afraid.

She probably should have been . . . after all, she was being kept a prisoner by a man bent on revenge, a man who was certainly her physical superior. She had read and shuddered over *The Collector*. She should have been terrified, spending every waking moment planning ways and means to escape. But she was not.

In a somewhat confused way she wondered if the escapade on the roof had not exorcised both her fear and her need to escape. Yet she did not really understand why. As day by day the slow hours ticked by, she could only conclude that for some unknown reason, it felt right to be where she was. Sean Reilly was of significance in her life. She knew that, knew it in her bones. What that would mean in the future, she had no idea. She only knew she did not want to escape. That she was content to wait upon events, to see what would happen, to let Sean take the initiative and follow his lead. Something would happen, of that she was certain, for intuitively she sensed that Sean was like her: he needed risk and the edge of danger, he would not be content to wait for ever. . . .

However, one can only read so much. At times when she was sure Sean was busy downstairs Caroline put on her shorts and T-shirt and exercised, jogging on the spot, doing sit-ups and knee bends as the grazes on her legs healed. Sometimes she simply stared out of the window at a view she had already memorised down to the last detail.

She had often wondered what it would be like to have a few days completely to herself without responsibility for anyone or anything else. Now she had it, although in circumstances stranger than any she could have imagined, and she found that it soon palled. She would have been all right if she could have gone outdoors, to walk in the wet woods or lie in the sun on the grass watching the light dance on the river. But confinement in a small space, however pleasantly decorated and comfortable and no matter how many books she had to read, was still confinement, and her latent claustrophobia flared into life. By the third night she was not sleeping well, her eyes overtired from staring at the page, her mind going round and round in circles. The fourth night she lay awake for two hours, staring up at the ghostly outline of the canopy, and finally switched the light back on and read until three in the morning, falling asleep with it still burning.

She did not hear the welcoming thud of Baron's tail on the floor when Sean got up, nor did she hear the tap on the door when Sean brought up her breakfast. Her tousled head buried under the pillow to shut out the light, the sheets tangled around her waist from all her tossing and turning, she slept on. The door opened and the man stood quietly in the aperture, his eyes drawn to the four-poster bed.

The early morning sun was streaming through the window to fall across the bed and its single occupant, falling warm on the long curve of her back and the graceful line of her outflung arm. She was not wearing the navy blue nightdress. Instead her only garments were the diminutive écru bra and panties she had paid for herself.

His eyes took in other details. The light still burning on the bedside table. The open book among the tangled covers. The lingering fragrance of her scent. He said flatly, his voice over-loud, 'Gabrielle, wake up.'

No response.

'Gabrielle, I've brought your breakfast.'

She stirred slightly, but only to bury her head further in the pillow. Carefully he put the tray down on the bureau, then walked over to the bed. The thin straps of her bra looked pale against the honey-gold of her tan; the smooth skin seemed to glow with a life of its own in the sunlight. He reached out his hand, hesitated for a long moment, then rested it on her shoulder, closing his fingers over the softness of flesh, the fragile bones.

For a moment everything was suspended: the sleeping girl, the black-haired man with the unreadable grey eyes, the shafts of dazzling light. Then the girl moved, muttering something fretfully under her breath as she rolled to face him, stretching as bonelessly as a cat.

Her breasts were firm and exquisitely shaped; wherever she had sunbathed, she had done it without a bra, for there was no break in the golden tan. Her belly was taut, narrowing to the navel and the jut of pelvic bones.

Still bending over her, the man repeated very quietly. 'Wake up.'

Caroline's eyes flew open. She stared at him uncomprehendingly, her mouth soft from sleep, her face, without make-up or adornment, reduced to the purity of its fine bones and dark velvet irises. She had been dreaming . . . she had been lying in the heat of the sun with a black-haired man. Was she awake now, or was the dream still continuing? Moving towards the inevitable act which she now knew she craved with all her heart? Was this why she had not been afraid, and had not wanted to escape?

She felt his weight on the mattress, saw his face come closer and closer until she was losing herself in the clouded grey eyes. Then there was the first, almost tentative, touch of his mouth against hers. She closed her eyes again, putting her arms around him as naturally as if they had done this many times before, and offering him her lips with confidence and generosity.

His full weight fell on her, his body heat replacing the warmth of the sun, burning into her flesh as the sun had never done. His kiss deepened, seeking from her a more complex response. She opened to him, her slender form convulsing in needs as old as the seasons, yet as new to her as the delicate green leaves of spring.

She could feel him along the whole length of her body. The hardness of his chest crushing her breasts, the dig of his belt buckle at her waist, and the awakening of his own need between her thighs. She had never been held like this before, never been kissed so comprehensively and hungrily until her head whirled and her body ached for more. She was at the top of a new slope, one never travelled before, and recklessly, joyously, she abandoned herself to all the excitement and danger of the descent. . . .

His hands had been smoothing her ribs and the concavity of her waist. Then she felt the move upwards and knew in her mind their destination before her body could signal the delicious shock of their arrival. Cupping her breasts, Sean began to stroke them, gently, repetitiously, while all the while his mouth plundered hers, their lips moulded together in an intimacy beyond anything Caroline could have imagined.

She was lost, betrayed by the body she had always controlled assaulted by the drive of a desire she had never before experienced. The slow, deliberate movement of his palms was driving her crazy; she fumbled for the closure of her bra, freeing her swollen breasts from that last confinement, wanting no impediment to the glorious, agonising touch of his hands. Instinctively she moved her hips against him, whimpering with pleasure deep in her throat.

Briefly he raised his head, separating his mouth from hers, his eyes devouring the flushed cheeks and trembling, parted lips, his breathing fast and hard. Then he levered himself up from her body, his gaze shifting to the golden, pink-topped breasts, as beautiful as flowers.

She lay very still, hearing her heart pound in her ears, knowing what he was about to do, her willing flesh quivering in anticipation. Lightly his tongue circled one nipple, the very heart of the rose, before he gathered the petal-soft skin into his mouth.

Arched against him, hands under his shirt digging into his spine, she cried out his name again and again, a litany of longing and pleasure, a wordless plea that he never stop. And then she heard him groan, 'Gabrielle ... oh God, you're so beautiful!' and the sun and the flowers vanished as if they had never been.

Frantically she pushed him away, her eyes crazed with hurt. 'I'm Caroline!' she gasped incoherently. 'Caroline—not Gabrielle! Oh, how could you call me Gabrielle?'

Sean reared up on one elbow, passion fading from his face, intelligence and awareness reasserting themselves. 'Because you are Gabrielle.'

'I'm not, I'm not!' Frantically she fumbled for her bra, trying to cover herself.

'If you didn't want to make love—and you could have fooled me, if ever a woman was willing, you were—why didn't you just say so? Instead of going through this charade again.'

His deliberate brutality appalled her. She whispered more to herself than to him, 'I did want to make love

. . . it's the first time in my life I've ever felt like that. But when I make love, I must know I'm wanted as myself. As Caroline. Not as another woman . . . surely you can understand that?' Dark as pansies, her eyes pleaded with him to agree with her.

His next words were like droplets of ice flung against her skin, shocking her back to all the realities she had been avoiding. 'Cut it out,' he said roughly, swinging his legs round and standing up beside the bed. 'You've slept with any number of men, Gabrielle, my own brother among them—so don't give me this terrified virgin act. It's scarcely appropriate.'

She lost any vestige of restraint in a searing pain that he could be so mistaken. 'So what were you trying to do?' she lashed back. 'Add yourself to the grand total?'

'Don't worry, I won't be doing that,' he answered grimly. 'You looked so beautiful when I came in, I let myself forget who you are. It won't happen again.' He jerked his head towards the bureau. 'Your breakfast's there.'

The glass of orange juice and the coffee mug looked disconcertingly normal. When she looked back, he was gone. In her ears the slam of the door echoed and re-echoed. She threw herself face down on the bed, her body racked by sobs, the tears soaking into the pillow. She didn't care if he heard her. She didn't care if she ever saw him again. She hated him, hated him, hated him. . . .

The next tap at the door came four hours later. Caroline had cried herself to sleep, had had a horrifying nightmare in which she was skiing out of control at top speed straight for a cliff, and had woken with her heart shaking her body and her face still wet with tears. In the bathroom she had done her best to repair the ravages of her crying spell, but the face she raised as the door opened was still tear-swollen. From her cross-legged perch on the bed, where she had been gazing sightlessly at the same page for nearly half an hour, she said rudely, 'What do you want?'

Sean shoved his hands in his pockets . . . hands that had caressed her breasts, she thought with a shiver. He looked none the worse for wear. No heart-searching there. No wondering how he had allowed himself to get involved sexually with a woman he despised. He only looked impatient, and anxious to be gone. He said, not bothering to sound anything but irritable, 'Lunch is ready——'

'I'm not hungry.'

He ignored her interruption. 'So why don't you come downstairs and eat in the kitchen with me?'

Caroline had spent at least an hour before he arrived wondering what on earth had happened to her earlier that morning, why she had responded so shamelessly, so wantonly, to a man whom she certainly did not love, perhaps did not even like. She had loved Richard. Yet she had never been in the slightest danger of being overcome by passion in Richard's presence. Why then did Sean Reilly have only to kiss her and she collapse in his arms, as willing as any of the girls whom she had privately despised years ago at the ski lodges: girls who had hopped from bed to bed as casually as they had changed their clothes. The storm of emotion that had overcome her when Sean had kissed her had been a revelation to Caroline, nor had she been able to come to terms with it. It was inexplicable. Only one thing was certain—it could not be repeated.

'No, thank you,' she said, trying to sound firm and only succeeding in sounding petulant.

'Come off it, Gabrielle. You know damn well you want to get out of this room, now don't you?'

'Of course I do. But not in your company.'

'Bitchy, bitchy,' he murmured, a malicious gleam in his eyes.

Incongruously she had an urge to laugh. She *was* being bitchy. And she did want to go downstairs and eat in the kitchen where she could look out over the river and see something other than grass and trees.

'Come on,' he coaxed. 'You know you want to.'

'Darn you!' she exploded. 'I'm furious with you and I'm just as angry with myself, and yes, I do want to.'

He threw back his head and laughed; it was the most contagious sound she had ever heard—besides making him look astonishingly youthful and devastatingly handsome. A reluctant smile tugged at her lips. 'You'd better have something good to eat after all this.'

'Homemade turkey soup and fresh rolls.'

'I guess that will do.' Her smile was wider now.

He stepped aside so she could leave the room ahead of him, and as she brushed past him to her nostrils came a tantalising reminder of the scent of his skin, clean and very masculine. Resolutely not looking at him, knowing she was blushing, she walked along the hall and down the stairs.

The table in the alcove had been set for two. Caroline said wryly, 'You're very sure of yourself.'

'In some matters, yes,' he replied cryptically. 'Others, less so. Why don't you serve the soup? The bowls are over there. I'll butter the rolls.'

For a moment she looked around the kitchen, bright and sunny, with no secrets or dark corners. The hanging begonias were in flower, their frilled pink and white petals with a pearl-like sheen. The copper pots twinkled in the sun, while the bunches of herbs scented the air faintly and subtly. *Parsley, sage, rosemary and thyme.* . . .

Unknown to her, Sean had been watching her. He said roughly, 'I've written out a synopsis of events the way I think they happened at the border—why don't you sign it, Gabrielle, and we'll bring this melodrama to an end. You don't like being a prisoner any more than I like being your jailer.'

The kitchen's deceptive peace was shattered. Caroline rounded on him like a fury. 'Allow me to tell you something, Sean Reilly,' she said tightly. 'I decided something this morning. I'm not answering to the name of Gabrielle any more.'

'So what am I supposed to call you?'

'What's wrong with Caroline? It's my name, after all.'

'I suppose I should give you full marks for persistence, if nothing else.'

She turned away, her eyes blurring unexpectedly with tears. Gabrielle was at best a liar, at worst a criminal . . . it hurt horribly to know that Sean still regarded her as either of those. Blindly she picked up a bowl and the big ladle, lifting the heavy cast-iron lid from the soup pot and putting it on the counter.

The soup was bubbling and steaming, and smelled delicious. She stirred it, for it was thick with barley, vegetables, and meat, then began to pour a ladleful into the first bowl. But she was still blinking back tears, not really watching what she was doing. A splash of the boiling liquid hit her thumb, she jerked her hand, and somehow there was soup all over her wrist and forearm, agonisingly hot.

Her gasp of pain and the clatter as the bowl struck the floor were almost simultaneous. Sean turned his head, grabbed her round the waist and pulled her to the sink, washing off the scalding vegetables under the cold tap, all without wasting a second. Then, with one look at her ashen face, he thrust her into a chair and lowered her head to her knees.

Someone was breathing shallowly, making tiny whimpers of pain. It took Caroline a full minute to realise it was herself. Her whole arm was burning, as if it was on fire, yet the rest of her felt very cold. Pushing back the dizziness, she tried to raise her head, dimly aware of the weight of Sean's hand on the back of her neck under her hair. 'I'm okay,' she whispered shakily.

He came round to kneel in front of her. 'Let me see your arm.'

She held it out, even that slight a movement bringing

sweat to her forehead. The skin was fiery red with tiny blisters where the vegetables had landed on it; the pain was excruciating. Sean said quietly, 'The skin isn't broken, so there shouldn't be any infection. Stay where you are a minute and I'll fill the sink with cold water—that'll help the pain.'

Stay where you are, he'd said. As if she had any choice, she thought with a desperate attempt at humour. She was quite sure her legs wouldn't hold her up. She bent her head, biting her lip to keep herself from moaning out loud.

It seemed a long time until Sean came back for her; she had made her lip bleed and the nails of her good hand were digging into the palm, but at least she was managing to keep silent. Had she been watching Sean, she would have seen besides the compassion in his face and kind of puzzlement deep in his eyes, as though something was not as he would have expected it to be. But she was concentrating on fighting back the waves of nausea and dizziness, and when he asked gently, 'Can you walk?' she merely nodded stoically.

Even through the pain she felt the comfort of having his arm around her as she wobbled her way to the sink. After the first shock of immersion, the cold water did gradually deaden the white-hot agony in her arm, particularly after Sean added some ice cubes to the water. Perched uncomfortably on a stool, she rested her forehead on her other hand and closed her eyes, shivering with cold and delayed shock.

She had no idea how much time passed before Sean said, 'I think that's done all the good it's going to do. I'll carry you into the living room and put a cold compress on your arm, and then I'll make you a cup of tea.'

Wordlessly she submitted, feeling herself being lifted, her sore arm away from his body. He was very strong, she thought muzzily, letting her head rest on his chest, the steady beat of his heart against her cheek. Even in the extremity of her pain, or perhaps because of it, she could think of nowhere she would rather be than in his arms. . . .

He lowered her to the chesterfield, adjusting a pillow under her head and bringing a blanket to cover her. The compress was cold, wet clothes surrounded by a dry towel; she tried not to flinch as he wrapped it around her wrist. Then he lit the fire and went back to the kitchen to make the tea.

Snuggled in the soft folds of the blanket, the pain mercifully abating, Caroline watched the dancing flames in the fireplace, her mind drifting aimlessly as she recalled the deftness of Sean's fingers on her wrist, the strength of his arms lifting her from the stool, the utter security of his embrace. When he came back in the room a few moments later, saying matter-of-factly, 'Tea'll be ready in a minute,' she murmured, 'Sean, come here.'

He sat on the edge of the couch. 'Is it still hurting?'

She put up her good arm and tugged at his shirtfront to bring his head down. 'Come here,' she repeated weakly. Then, as he lowered his face to hers, a quizzical expression on it, she kissed him full on the mouth. 'Thank you,' she said.

She had never seen him look quite as he did then, and she would have been at a loss to describe the sequence of emotions that chased each other across his features. 'Gabri——' he began, then broke off, raking his hand through his thick black hair. 'Hell, I don't even know what to call you, let alone who you are. I wish to God I did know——'

Pain, and now the miraculous alleviation of it, had removed any inhibitions Caroline might have had. She wanted to touch him and never let him go . . . she rested her fingers lightly on his bare forearm, through her fingertips feeling a current of awareness course through her whole body. 'I'm Caróline,' she said simply.

'If I hadn't been arguing with you about just that, maybe you wouldn't have spilled the soup.'

'Please—don't blame yourself. It was my fault, I was clumsy,' she said, distressed.

He smoothed the hair back from her forehead. 'Who *are* you?' he said very quietly.

I'm the woman who's in love with you. For a moment she thought she had said the words out loud; her eyes widened and her lips parted. 'I—I could ask the same of you.'

'How well can we even know ourselves? Let alone someone else,' was the enigmatic response.

She blurted, 'Sean, are you married?'

She had caught both of them by surprise. 'No. What makes you ask?'

'I don't know. I just wondered.'

'No. It's something I've always shied away from. Never felt ready for it. Or else I've never met the right woman.'

You've met her now, she wanted to cry. *But you think she's someone else, someone you despise.*

'And you?'

'Oh—no.'

'Why not?' But the grey eyes had clouded, and the presence of Martin was between them as palpably as if he had been standing there.

'Never been asked,' she said flippantly. 'The tea will be cold.'

'It will, won't it?' Slowly he got to his feeet, looking down at her, a frown marring his forehead. 'If only I could know who you are. . . .'

'Maybe you'll have to decide. Make a choice. I'm either Gabrielle or Caroline—I can't be both.'

'A woman can have many faces. And who is to say which is the true one?' he answered evasively.

Caroline summoned all her energy, knowing she was fighting for something that was desperately important. 'You have to trust your senses, what you see and hear. And then decide which is the true face.'

He looked at her, his expression inscrutable. 'You're right, of course. Although it's not quite as easy as you make it sound . . . I'll get the tea.'

Caroline let out her breath in a long sigh as he left the room, feeling exhaustion wash over her. The flames leaped and danced, melding into an incandescent orange ball, all heat and light . . . her lashes drifted to her cheeks and her breathing deepened. When Sean came back into the room, she was asleep. For several long minutes he stood watching her, his eyes lingering on the ivory-pale skin, the blue shadows under the thick lashes, the vulnerable curve of mouth; his fists were clenched at his sides, the frown very much in evidence. The flames had died to glowing red coals by the time he picked up a book from the coffee table and went to sit by the window to read, his vision angled so he could always see the sleeping girl on the couch.

When Caroline woke, it was early evening. She was not in bed; the pillows were too yielding for that, the blanket too soft and fleecy. So where was she? She opened her eyes, feeling a shaft of pain lance her forehead at the brightness of the light, and blinking to clear her vision.

'How are you? You've slept a long time.'

Sean. Sitting in the chair against the light. 'I've got an awful headache,' she mumbled, trying to sit up, then falling back with a tiny cry as she jarred her burned arm.

'Maybe you should be in bed,' he said calmly. 'How does that sound?'

'All right. I'm sorry I'm being such a nuisance.'

'You're not being a nuisance,' he said, and something in this understated reply reassured her as loud protestations would not have.

He pulled the blanket off her and lifted her very carefully, carrying her up the stairs, Baron plodding behind them.

'Bathroom first,' Caroline muttered.

'Okay. Don't lock the door, and call if you need me.'

In the bathroom Caroline took one look at herself in the mirror and winced away from her own reflection. She looked like a ghost, she thought uncharitably, her eyes sunk in her head, her cheeks paper-white. The throbbing in her arm and the throbbing in her temples seemed indistinguishable; to put it mildly, she felt wretched.

When she left the bathroom she had to call for Sean, knowing she could not negotiate the expanse of bare floor by herself. He had already turned down the bed; the crisp white sheets looked very inviting. She sat down on the edge of the mattress, trying to sound convincing as she said, 'I'll be all right now.'

'Where's your nightdress?'

'It's still in the bag. I-I haven't worn it.' Remembering how he had found her in bed—had it only been this morning?—and what had happened, a tinge of colour crept into her cheeks.

He found it in the paper bag beside the bureau and pulled it out, snapping off the tags. 'But you'll wear it now, won't you?' he asked, and with one part of her brain she noticed how scrupulously he was avoiding calling her anything, Gabrielle or Caroline.

She had neither the energy nor the desire to refuse him. She nodded, adding faintly, 'You'd better turn your back.'

'Don't be silly,' he said prosaically. 'Pretend I'm your brother or your father or something.'

Through the pounding in her head she heard herself say, 'I could never do that, Sean.'

It stopped him dead, his hand already on her T-shirt, his face very close to hers. 'No . . . I don't think either of us can pretend that, can we?' His lips brushed her cheek and rested very briefly on her mouth. Then he moved back a little, saying with deliberate casualness, 'We'll take the shirt over your good arm first.'

Getting the tight-fitting shirt off was the worst part;

by the time he had eased it over her burned skin, Caroline was shaking. But one look at Sean's face told her he was minding it as much as she; he was white about the mouth, his jaw set. She stood up while he slid her jeans down over her hips. And then he was undoing her bra, his fingers warm on her flesh, and she could not have said whether she was trembling from pain or pleasure. With infinite gentleness he cupped the firm, silk-smooth flesh in his hands, then lowered his head to rest in the valley between them.

Of its own volition Caroline's hand came up to hold his head there, her fingers buried in the thick black hair, while dimly she wondered if she would faint with sheer delight. When he straightened, very slowly as if he did not want to, he must have seen the wonderment in the velvet eyes; he kissed her again, still without saying a word, and slid the nightdress over her head.

The fabric, as dark blue as her eyes, clung to her breasts and hips before flaring to the floor; the design left her shoulders, arms, and the cleft between her breasts bare, and in its very severity was seductive in a way frills and lace might not have been. Sean said huskily, 'You look very beautiful.' His mouth quirked. 'And very tired. Lie down, and I'll cover you.'

Unable to think of anything to say, she did as she was told. He adjusted an extra pillow under her sore arm, then pulled the covers up to her chin. 'I'll leave the door open. Sleep well, and call if you need me.'

It was the second time he had said that. *I do need you*, she cried inwardly. *I need you as I have never needed a man before*. But how could she tell him that?

'I will,' she said meekly. Avoiding looking at him again, she let her cheek fall sideways on the pillow and gave herself up to sleep.

CHAPTER SIX

IN the morning Caroline felt like a new woman; sleep had been what she needed. Her arm, while still tender to touch, had lost the angry redness in the skin, and she could move it without the sharp pain of the day before.

She got up and showered, then managed to get dressed, although drying her hair proved unexpectedly difficult: a task for which one took two hands for granted. Wearing shorts and the yellow T-shirt, for the sun was shining again, she went back into her room, gazing wistfully out of the window at the tall grass, sprinkled with daisies and orange hawkweed, and at the green canopy of the trees. She'd like to be out there, letting the sun warm her face and dry her hair. . . .

There had been no sign of either Sean or Baron when she had got up. Now she heard the sound of footsteps taking the stairs two at a time, and turned towards the door as Sean came down the hallway. 'How are you feeling?' he said abruptly.

He was wearing a faded pair of denim shorts, fraying at the hem, and nothing else. She swallowed, taking refuge in politeness. 'Much better, thank you.'

'Let me see your arm.'

In three quick strides he had reached her, lifting her arm to the light and examining the area of the burn. 'Looks a lot better, doesn't it? Can't you dry your hair?'

'It'll dry eventually.'

'Come on outside and I'll do it for you.'

Again, no name. Was she being a fool to interpret that as a good sign? 'You mean I can go out?'

His grey eyes giving nothing away, he said, 'You still look pale. It'll do you good to get out in the sun.'

'You're not scared I'll try and run away again?' she

said provocatively, suddenly wanting to know what he was thinking.

His eyes narrowed. 'You'd get no further than you did the last time.'

He was right, of course. In silence she preceded him down the stairs and out the front door, determined to keep her distance; she had woken up remembering what had happened the evening before and had blushed at her own behaviour. She had encouraged him blatantly—which did not mean she had to do the same thing today. But when she stepped outside and felt the first touch of the morning sun on her face and heard the birds calling back and forth in the trees and the distant murmur of the river, she could not have stopped herself from saying, 'Mmm . . . what a *beautiful* day!'

'Isn't it?' Sean indicated the lawn furniture. 'Sit down over there and I'll get a towel and a comb.'

The grass tickled the soles of her feet; it was a gloriously vivid green. Across the limpid blue sky a group of gulls soared and wheeled, catching the sun on their wings and snow-white breasts. She found herself studying the dandelions, marvelling at the intricate geometry of their ragged yellow faces as if she had never seen one before. Perhaps she never really had, she decided thoughtfully. She had taken them for granted, and it had taken a week of solitude to make her appreciate them. A sobering thought.

She was sitting on one of the weathered grey benches that overlooked the river's deep ravine when Sean came back out. He had slung the towel, a white one, over his shoulder, where it made his hair look as black as coal and his tan like bronze, and with her new clarity of vision she wondered if she would ever again see anything as beautiful as this man walking across the grass towards her. That proudly held head had rested against her breasts; the lean, elegant hands had brought her pleasure beyond belief. She wanted the moment to last for ever, so that he would be always coming towards her and she waiting for him. . . .

'What are you looking at me like that for? Have I got shaving cream on my chin?'

'N-no. I—everything just seems especially beautiful to me today after being cooped up indoors,' Caroline said lamely, then blushed in case he realised she was also referring to him.

'Lean your head forward.'

Glad to hide her face, she bent over. He began drying her hair, his fingers digging into her scalp, and she gave herself up to it, glad that he was near her, glad to be where she was. Something was happening to her, she thought confusedly, something compared to which her relationship with Richard had been only a pale shadow. A few days ago when she had first met Sean she had had the sensation of being balanced at the very top of the slope in that nerve-wrenching moment when time itself was suspended. But now she was descending, headlong, faster and faster, to a destination unknown to her: a finishing line where she might be either winner or loser, she had no way of telling. She had the strange intuition that the prize was more to be desired than anything she had ever achieved; equally, were she to lose, that her life would never be the same again.

'There,' Sean said casually, bringing her back to reality with a start. 'Put your head up.'

She stared straight at his chest as he combed her hair back from her face, feeling the tug and stroke of the teeth with a tiny shiver of delight. Her hair would be curling around her ears and the nape of her neck after being towelled dry, she knew: a coiffure very different from Gabrielle's sleek style.

When he had finished, Sean put the comb and the towel on the bench and sat down on the grass at her feet, facing her. All her defences down, her face relaxed and softened by the myriad beauties of the morning, she smiled at him gravely. But the smile was wiped from her face by his next words. 'Tell me about this Caroline Travers,' he said deliberately. 'Where does she live, what does she do, does she have any brothers and sisters? I want to know about her.'

Her throat suddenly dry, Caroline swallowed the instinctive question that rose to her lips. *Why?* she wanted to ask. *Why do you want to know?*

But that one little three-letter word might shatter the mood between them, might drive him back into his shell. He had asked the question—that was enough.

Leaning forward, her gaze fixed on the slow, powerful current of the river, she said dreamily, 'Caroline . . . born in New Brunswick twenty-two years ago. Parents both doctors, eldest of the family, one younger sister and seventeen-year-old twin brothers. Identical twins, who get themselves into and out of mischief with truly astonishing regularity.' Her smile broke through. 'They're going to be let loose on the Dalhousie campus this fall—I shudder to think of the results! But to get back to Caroline . . . she hated school because they make you sit still in nice little desks in tidy rows. Not her thing. Started off in figure skating, but that wasn't——' she paused, head on one side as she sought for the right word, 'risky enough. Switched to skiing, and fell in love with it.' Her face softened, her eyes seeing, instead of the river, the slopes at Wentworth where she had first learned to ski.

'I took to it like a duck to water,' she went on, not even noticing how she had changed from the third person to the first. 'As long as I could spend every weekend and a couple of evenings a week on skis, even school became bearable. Anyway, I wasn't allowed to go to skiing if my marks weren't over seventy-five, my parents saw to that. They never really understood the fascination the slopes had for me, the exhilaration of the speed . . . but they were wise enough to let me do it.'

The man was watching her intently, a look of puzzlement hidden deep in the grey eyes. He had

noticed the change in person, and saw every flicker of
expression in the vivid, mobile face. He might have had
questions; if so, he forbore to ask them.

'Well, the inevitable happened. I started winning
races—local ones first, then district, then provincial. I
went through three coaches in three years and finally
was accepted by Canada's top downhill coach. I could
do slalom and giant slalom, but downhill was my forte.
The precision, the balance, the importance of every
fraction of a second. I loved it. I became a member of
the national team and started doing the international
circuits. At nineteen I was placed seventh in the winter
Olympics. And then I started moving up. Fifth place,
fourth, bronze medallion, silver. Val d'Isère, Kitzbühel,
St Anton, Sarajevo. Everywhere I went, I got better. I
was headed for the top and I knew it. I wanted to win
everything there was to win . . . I did defeat the reigning
Swiss champion, twice. I've always been glad of that.'

'What happened?'

The question was so quietly spoken it hardly even
disturbed the flow of her narrative. 'It was in Sarajevo
two winters ago. It's a short course but a tough one.
There's a series of giant slalom turns, where if you went
wide, you'd had it. Then on the triple bumps near the
finish line you'd lose time if your skis left the ground.
It's a bald mountain, open to the wind and the weather,
so you never knew from one moment to the next what
to expect. Capricious was a word the commentators
used to use there a lot. The other thing they used to say
was how Travers of Canada always skied on the edge of
destruction. And so I did. It was the way to win.'

'I was top seed that day, and drew the last position at
the gate. The course was treacherous, a lot of ice. The
Swiss girl had a better time than I'd had in practice
runs, and because I was hell-bent on beating her, I
knew I'd have to clip the turns to the maximum. So I
did, and for the first four it worked. I *knew* my time
was good. I was doing about fifty miles an hour at the

fifth, I suppose, hit a patch of ice, went out of control, and crashed into the fence. Multiple breaks in my right leg, four months in traction, and a permanent weakness in the joint.'

'No more skiing.'

'No more competitive skiing, certainly. I had a hard time for a while, because I'd made it my whole life, and so I was left with a vacuum. Nothing. But I'd also known all along that accidents happen and that's the risk.' She grimaced. 'The Swiss girl won the European championship again that year, too. She wouldn't have, if I'd still been around.'

Sean laughed. 'I bet she wouldn't! So what next?'

'My parents were wonderful—left me alone for just long enough, and then proposed a new challenge. They'd finance the purchase of a small business for me, but after that it would be up to me to make a success of it. I'd always been a great reader, so I bought a bookstore in Halifax. I made enough profit last year to pay off forty per cent of the debts. So it's getting there.'

'And is she married, this Caroline Travers? Or engaged?'

There was a note in Sean's voice that brought Caroline back to the present with a jolt. She said shortly, 'Neither.'

'Not even in love?'

Too close to the bone by far. 'No.'

'Not a challenge you're interested in?'

'Not a risk I want to take.'

'I find that hard to believe,' he said smoothly. 'The girl who always skies on the edge of destruction and has created a profitable business in these days of competition and inflation would hardly be a virgin.'

She flushed scarlet. 'First, that's not what you asked. And secondly, it's none of your business.'

'I think it is. Because it's many years since Gabrielle abandoned any pretence at chastity.'

'What a very old-fashioned word,' she mocked, praying the hurt did not show.

'As is virginity these days.'

'And what about you?' she flailed. 'Are you a virgin, Sean Reilly?'

'No, I'm not.'

The thought of him with another woman filled her with an emotion that could only be jealousy. 'Do I detect a double standard?'

'At least I'm honest about it—Gabrielle.'

She stood up, the sun gilding her heaving breasts and her long, slender legs in the brief shorts. 'I'm not Gabrielle—I'm Caroline!'

'*Tu penses que je le crois? Tu n'es rien qu'une putain!*'

Far too upset to notice that he had spoken French, and understanding all too well every word he had said, she spat back, '*Tais-toi! Je ne veux plus entendre.*'

There was a dead silence, into which a thrush dropped its lilting, liquid song, incredibly beautiful, totally unnoticed by either of them. Sean got up, standing two or three feet away from her, his face a frozen mask. Contempt was to be read there, she thought numbly. But underlying that was something else. Pain? Disillusion? What was it?

'You do realise what you've just done?' he said heavily. 'You didn't even notice when I switched to French ... because it's your native tongue, isn't it, Gabrielle?'

She raised her chin, her dark eyes steady. 'The ski coach I mentioned, who was my coach for three years, was from Quebec and spoke no English. So I learned to speak French, to joke and swear in French, to think in French.'

She knew he would not believe her, nor did he. 'You have an answer for everything, don't you? I'm going into the house. You can do what you like. Guard, Baron.'

Her emotions in a turmoil of mingled fury that he

could be so obtuse and pain that he could be so
distrustful, Caroline watched him go, knowing with
shame that she wanted to call him back, to beg him to
believe her. It was partly pride that prevented her,
partly the certainty that it would do no good.

When he had disappeared into the house, she sat
down with a thud on the bench. 'Baron,' she said out
loud, 'what am I going to do? I thought he was starting
to accept me. At least to realise I'm different from
Gabrielle. And now look—it's as bad as it ever was.
Oh, damn ...' The dog watched her unblinkingly, his
nose on his paws. 'You're no good,' she quavered.
'You're on his side, aren't you?' The thick tail swept the
grass in agreement.

Eventually Caroline spread the towel on the ground
and lay in the sun, trying not to think about anything.
At noon Sean came out to get her. 'Lunch is ready,' he
said coldly. 'Then you'd better go back to your room.'

Like a naughty child who's being punished ... not
deigning to answer, she stalked past him, the effect
rather spoiled when she stubbed her bare toe on a rock.
Lunch was cold turkey sandwiches, iced tea, and fruit;
picking hers up, she said crisply, 'Thank you,' and went
upstairs with it, ostentatiously shutting the door of her
room. The first thing she saw was the philosophy book,
all six hundred closely printed pages of it. Glaring at it
balefully, she sat down on the bed and began to eat.

She was acting rather like a spoiled child, she thought
ruefully. But she had no idea how else to behave.
Honesty, and the sharing of true experiences, had got
her nowhere. *Make love to him*, a little voice whispered
in her brain. *Then he'll know you're not Gabrielle.*

On this very bed he had kissed and caressed her,
bringing to life a new Caroline, a passionate and hot-
blooded woman whom she had not even known existed.
He only did it because he thought you were easy, a
cynical voice sneered bck.

The sandwiches suddenly tasted like sawdust. Picking

up the philosophy book, she read at random, 'The basis of modern idealism is Kant's doctrine of the Transcendental ego of Apperception.' No help there. Flinging it across the bed, she ended up sleeping away the afternoon, waking around five-thirty heavy-eyed and bad-tempered.

It was cooler in the room now, so Caroline changed into jeans and Gabrielle's silk shirt. As she was doing it up, she paused halfway, her face very thoughtful, her mouth starting to lift in a smile. Then she deliberately left the top buttons open to expose the cleavage between her breasts, and began making up her face with more than a touch of exaggeration. Blusher dramatically heightened her cheekbones; two applications of mascara and three toning shades of eyeshadow made her eyes look huge. She brushed her hair back from her ears, fastening it with two gold clips that she had found in the bottom of Gabrielle's bag, and letting a tumble of curls fall forward over her forehead. She surveyed the results in the mirror with considerable satisfaction: if she was going to be taken as a floozy, she might as well look the part. She thrust her hips forward, pouted her lips, and smouldered seductively at her own reflection.

She had just finished painting her toe nails scarlet and putting on Gabrielle's expensive sandals, when she heard footsteps and then Sean's voice at the door. 'Dinner's ready. You might as well eat downstairs.'

She pulled the door open smartly, the pout rather spoiled by an urge to giggle as she saw him blink in surprise. 'May I really? You're sure I won't ruin your appetite?'

He had recovered himself, and very slowly let his eyes wander over her from head to foot, lingering on the décolletage of her shirt. 'My appetite for what?' he drawled.

Her cheeks pink from more than blusher, she spat a very rude French word at him, but he only grinned appreciatively. 'This looks like open warfare.'

'If I'm to be judged as Gabrielle, I might as well look the part.'

'You're succeeding beyond your wildest dreams.'

It was very hard to resist that glimmer of amusement in his eyes; she had expected him to be angry, not entertained. She should have known by now that it was impossible to anticipate how he would react; she should also have known that he would always remain one jump ahead of her. But it did have the effect of heightening the challenge, no question of it. She gave him the full benefit of a very provocative smile and sauntered down the stairs ahead of him, hips swaying in the skin-tight jeans.

The table was set in the alcove. Moving unhurriedly, Sean lowered the split bamboo blinds over the tall expanse of window and took two candles out of a drawer. 'Why don't you go and put some—er—suitable music on in the living room?' he suggested urbanely.

She looked at him from under her lashes, she hoped with devastating effect. 'Certainly.'

The slope was getting steeper, she thought with a faint qualm at her own audacity, as she knelt by the shelf of records and started to thumb through them, knowing she was not at all in the mood for Bach, Beethoven, or Brahms. Louis Armstrong, maybe, or Scott Joplin. Then her eyes lit up. She pulled out the sleeve and put the record on the turntable, carefully picking the right cut. Volume up high, and then back to the kitchen, her expression all wide-eyed innocence.

Even in the kitchen the words were crystal clear. *That's why the lady is a tramp.* . . . 'Will that do?' she asked.

Like two fencers they faced each other across the table, now supplied with a bottle of Châteauneuf du Pape and two crystal wine glasses. 'An excellent choice.'

The meal, as usual, was delicious: pepper steak with sautéed onions, green peppers, and mushrooms, as well as baked stuffed tomatoes and a spinach salad. Passing her the basket of hot rolls, Sean took the offensive. 'How much did Martin tell you about me, Gabrielle?'

Her hand hesitated for only a second. 'As I've never met Martin, that's an impossible question to answer.'

'Allow me to rephrase it, then. What do you know about me?'

Thoughtfully she spread butter on the roll, wondering just how to respond. She looked up, the candlelight darkening her eyes to black, and said slowly, 'I think you're an adventurer. You're like me—you need risk, challenge, excitement. I'd be willing to bet you don't have a nine-to-five job, I'm sure you've been in any number of tight spots in your life, and I'm equally sure you've travelled in places I've probably never even heard of.'

'So he did tell you something.'

'I don't need anyone else to tell me that.' She suddenly dropped her eyes, unable to stand the intensity of his stare, and almost frightened by her own words. They were the literal truth . . . but where did this almost instinctual knowledge of him come from? And what did it signify?

'Tell me more.'

She cut a cube of meat with as much care as if it were an exercise in geometry. 'You can be ruthless, but not deliberately cruel. Frustrated and impatient, but still very much in control of your anger.' Her voice died to a whisper. 'Passionate, but gentle.'

In the other room the music had come to an end. A drop of wax sputtered on one of the candles. 'You seem to know rather a lot about me. I hadn't credited you with quite as much—sensitivity. Or perspicacity.'

She said, nervously crumbling the roll in fingers whose nails were red as blood, 'I've never actually heard anyone use that word before. Perspicacity, I mean. It was all guesswork, Sean.'

'Inspired guesswork,' he said dryly.

So what had she done? By once again sticking to the

truth, had she only served to convince Sean even more strongly that she was Gabrielle Cartier, intimate of his brother Martin? Unaware that something close to despair had dimmed her features, she said in a low voice, 'Why don't you give me your side of the story then? If you don't like guesswork, deal in facts.'

'Oh, facts,' he said impatiently. 'They're easy enough. Sean Jonathan Reilly, thirty-four years old, Canadian-born of Irish parents. One brother, Martin. No sisters, no wife, no children. No house, no place I call my own.' He drained his wine glass, refilling hers and his own, then raising his glass so that the candle flame glowed in its heart like a ruby. 'To independence, of which I have my fair share—as do you.'

'I was fortunate. I always knew my parents loved me, yet they allowed me all the freedom I could handle. There's a saying to the effect that if you love something, set it free, and it will come back to you. I guess I really believe that. Did your parents do the same?'

'My parents, bless their hearts, knew nothing but poverty until they came to Canada. Once here, they prospered, which was fine. But unfortunately the prosperity became an end in itself. Security, comfort, cold hard cash, became their gods, and I suppose my whole adult life has been a reaction against that. I've tested racing cars, I worked for a detective agency for a while, I've done a lot of solo trips for yacht designers, I run a charter company in the West Indies ... and it's only lately that I've begun to feel a need to settle, to put down roots and build.' He looked around at the shadowed, pleasant kitchen. 'This place, for instance. It belongs to friends of mine, who are chartering one of my sloops for a month while I have the use of the house. It has its attractions, doesn't it?'

'I think you'd rather be by the sea, though.'

He grinned, the sombre look vanishing from his face. 'You're right! I have it in my mind to start my own boatyard. Over the years I've picked up a lot of knowledge about boat design, and I'd like to put some of it to use.' He shrugged. 'I'll never be rich, that's not one of my aims. And I'll never work for someone else. What I do want to preserve is at least the illusion of freedom.'

Caroline understood completely. Raising her own glass, she said seriously, 'To the Reilly Boatyard, and the beautiful yachts you will launch there.'

He drank, his eyes as impenetrable as the sea he loved. '*Merci beaucoup, Gabrielle.*'

She had completely forgotten the game she was playing. Giving a brittle laugh, she tossed her head. '*Pas de quoi. Maintenant j'ai besoin de la musique. Nous sommes trop sérieux.*' Pushing away from the table, she fled into the living room. The other side of the musical, and the Canadian Brass playing ragtime: that would do.

She straightened, noticing for the first time through the wide picture windows how the sunset had splashed orange on the river and had dipped the gulls in ink as they flew, silhouetting them against the fading sky. *I'm in love with him*, she thought dazedly. *He's the man I was really looking for when I found Richard. He's the man I've been waiting for all my life.* The one man who would make her complete, whose soul matched her own ... she shivered suddenly, oppressed by the glowering sky and the angry death of the sun.

Her abrupt departure from the table had broken the mood between them; they talked of commonplaces during the rest of the meal, cleaned up the kitchen, and then moved to the living room with their coffee.

Caroline perched on the edge of one of the armchairs, already wishing she had gone straight to her room. She could think of nothing to say that was either intelligent or witty; she was certainly unable to relax. Her fingers were itching to do up at least one of the buttons on her blouse, but she knew Sean would notice and would draw his own conclusions, and she lacked the courage for another confrontation. All she wanted was to be called Caroline, she thought wretchedly, taking a cautious sip of the coffee, for it was very hot. A week ago that would have been a simple enough wish. Now it had assumed the proportions of an obsession.

She took another mouthful of coffee, deciding to go to her room when it was finished, for solitude was preferable to this strained silence between two people who had exposed facets of their personalities to each other and were not regretting it.

Sean had been changing the records to some dance music while she sat there. He could not know that she loved to dance; the inescapable conclusion was that Gabrielle must like it. Every way she turned she was brought face to face with Gabrielle, she realised with a rush of excitement. When Sean came to stand in front of her, holding out his hand, she said coldly, 'I don't want to dance.'

His answer was to pull her to her feet. She glared up at him. 'Don't, Sean.'

With exaggerated care he brought the arm she had burned up to his shoulder. Keeping her other hand in his, he encircled her waist. 'There's nothing wrong with this, is there?'

There were only inches between them; she could see the pulse throbbing at the base of his throat and from his hands a current of tingling awareness flowed through her whole body. She scarcely knew which to fear more: him, or her own reactions. And then he began to dance, and blindly she followed his lead, stumbling a little at first, her body stiff and awkward. But the music, a lushly orchestrated waltz, coupled with his physical proximity won her over, as she had known they would. She grew pliant in his arms, while the colour came back to her cheeks and her eyes began to sparkle.

From a waltz they went to a jive, and the last of Caroline's inhibitions fled. The sheer joy of movement and the pulsing rhythm of the music would have been enough; added to this was the sharp edge of risk, because both of them, she was sure, were all too aware of the undercurrent of sexuality as they touched and separated, whirled and swayed.

It was years since she had danced a tango; giggling at her own mistakes, she made a parody of it. And then it was another waltz, slower this time, infinitely more seductive. Sean drew her closer, pressing her lips to his throat, letting his cheek rest on her hair. She surrendered herself to his embrace with a tiny sigh, letting her mouth slide along the hard tendons of his neck, feeling his hand clasp her hips. Achingly aware of the whole length of his body so close to hers, she felt her breasts tingle and the nipples grow taut, and wondered dimly if he knew what was happening to her.

He must have, for he gave up any pretence of dancing. His hands moved to her waist, pulling the shirt free from her jeans and unbuttoning it. Caroline stood immobile, helpless to protest, as he unclasped her bra. Before she realised his intention, he was sliding both garments from her shoulders. In a rustle of cloth they fell to the floor.

She pulled back, sure that her heartbeat would suffocate her. 'Sean, no——'

He took her hands in his, guiding them to his chest. 'Take off my shirt,' he said huskily.

How could she refuse him, when deep within her she did not want to? Fumbling a little, she undid the buttons one by one, his eyes holding hers captive. It was he who undid the wristbands and impatiently shrugged the shirt off. Then it was he who very slowly drew her nearer until just the tips of her breasts brushed his skin. He must have seen how she quivered at the contact, her lips parting. His hands began to stroke the curves of her flesh as his mouth claimed hers in a kiss that demanded all the passion that was hers to give.

The gentle, repetitive movements of his fingers melted any resistance she might have had in a fire that gathered her whole body into its heart; the throb of his manhood against her thigh only fanned the flames. Devoured by his mouth, ravaged by his hands, she swayed against him, mindlessly wanting more of him, all he had to give.

Her hands had moved to his body, in touching innocence exploring the symmetry of muscle and bone that was so totally and overwhelmingly male. He grew still when she touched him, as though his whole attention was concentrating on her shy, tentative movements. Releasing her mouth, he moved back a little, his eyes watching her fingers move up his chest to entwine themselves in the tangled hair. In the darkened room her breasts had an exquisite pallor. Sean bent and kissed one, then the other, then clasped her arms, his quickened breathing echoing in her ears.

'I want you,' he said hoarsely, 'as I swear I've never wanted a woman before. Yet I can't even call you by name, can I? I want to call you Caroline, God knows I do. But something holds me back every time.'

She had not a vestige of pride left. 'Make love to me,' she whispered. 'Caroline is a virgin. Gabrielle, you say, is not.'

'Far from it, I'm sure,' and that ugly note was in his voice as it always was when he referred to the French girl. 'A very experienced and sophisticated lady, our Gabrielle. But also a born deceiver. She certainly fooled Martin.'

'*I'm* not like that.'

Sean suddenly turned away from her, going over to the window to stand gazing out, shoulders hunched, one fist banging at the frame over and over again, all his pent-up frustration in the thud of flesh on wood. 'I don't think I can take much more of this,' he muttered finally. 'And if you're Gabrielle, this will really make you laugh—I feel as though I'm being torn apart. I want to believe you. I want to believe you're as honest and as innocent as you appear to be.' He gave a short laugh that was devoid of humour. 'Innocent ...

scarcely the word I'd use for Gabrielle. And then I think of Martin locked up in that cell and it's as if he's standing between us the whole time.'

Caroline bent and picked up the silk shirt, pulling it on to cover her breasts but not bothering to do it up. 'I've felt that, too,' she said softly. 'I do understand, Sean. But I wish it were otherwise.' Her quietly spoken words brought him round to face her; she was shocked by the pain ravaging his face, the sunken eyes, and instinctively stepped closer, resting her hand lightly on his arm, feeling the tension in the bunched muscles. 'There's nothing I can do, is there?' she said helplessly. 'I can only be myself.' Her eyes were suddenly swimming with tears, and she blinked them back. 'I want you to *know* that I'm Caroline. To be sure of it, without the shadow of a doubt.'

'Caroline's different from Gabrielle,' he said, each word dragged from him. 'Independent and courageous, unawakened. Like the first flower of spring waiting for the touch of the sun to bring it to life.' He made a move towards her, then checked it in mid-air, his mouth a tormented line. His hands fell to his sides. 'If I touch you again, we'll both have had it,' he said with an attempted lightness that did not quite succeed.

There was no need for her to reply, for she knew he had said nothing but the truth. Fastening her shirt, she stooped to pick his up, passing it to him in silence.

'Thank you.' Then he said her name almost experimentally, as if trying out the sound of it on his tongue. 'Caroline. It's a pretty name.'

She sought for something, anything, to say that would relieve the emotional tension in the room. 'My father calls me Caro.'

'Maybe that's what I should call you ... the fine art of compromise. It's better than Gabby.'

Caroline actually managed a laugh. 'Anything would be better than that!'

'So it's a truce.'

'Very well,' she agreed gravely.

He ran his fingers through his hair. 'I'm going out for a walk, I need to be by myself for a while. 'I'll see you tomorrow.'

How often after a hard day's competition she had longed for solitude rather than the boisterous crowds in the ski chalets. 'All right. Goodnight, Sean.'

'Goodnight ... Caro.'

Feeling as tired as if she had indeed skied all day, Caroline trailed up the stairs. She should have been feeling happy, for surely there had been at least the beginning of some kind of resolution this evening. And she was in no doubt that he wanted her. Why then this leaden weight dogging her steps? This inexplicable feeling of depression? He had called her Caro, hadn't he? He had even said her real name. That should be enough. . . .

CHAPTER SEVEN

STALEMATE.

That was the only word Caroline could find to describe the next few days. She was forced to conjecture that on his solitary walk Sean had decided to back away from any further personal involvement with her, a decision that must mean he was still unsure of her identity, wavering between Caroline, to whom he was attracted, and Gabrielle, whom he hated.

He was polite. At mealtimes he talked effortlessly about any number of subjects, a tactic that ensured they stayed away from personal matters. The rest of the time he simply absented himself, leaving her to Baron and her own devices. She read. She exercised, She listened to music. And the slow summer days drifted by, days of mist and rain, days of sunshine and fluffy white clouds and crisp breezes that teased the surface of the river into lace-edged ruffles.

She had never been a very patient person, a characteristic that had been of benefit in her drive to excel at skiing. But now it did not stand her in good stead. Each day she could feel the tension mounting a little higher, the tightening of her nerves when Sean was near her, the frustration when he was not. Not that his physical presence was of much benefit. He very carefully kept a distance between them; he never touched her; not by the flicker of an eye did he reveal that it made any difference to him whether she was there or not.

By the weekend her nerves had reached the screaming point. Had she been Gabrielle, she thought wryly, she would undoubtedly have signed any number of confessions. As she was not, she was left with the alternative of forcing some kind of a confrontation.

Anything that would make Sean look at her as if she was at least real, a creature of flesh and blood who had a name.

It had been the tacit understanding all along that she stay indoors, and up until now she had not challenged this rule. But after five days of virtually being ignored, she was in the mood to challenge anything. After breakfast, a meal eaten with very little conversation because they were listening to the radio, Sean went outside and Baron padded out into the front hall to lie in a patch of sunshine on the carpet. Caroline finished putting away the dishes in the kitchen. The weather office was forecasting a storm for the following day, the fringe of a hurricane due to pass south of them, and her mouth set in a mutinous line. Be damned if she was going to stay meekly indoors all day! The sun was shining and she wanted to go out, particularly if it was going to rain tomorrow. She she would go out. And to hell with Sean Reilly!

She knew she would have to be fast if she didn't want Baron following her. Sneaking a look into the hall, she saw the big dog stretched out asleep, the sun glistening on his coat. Back in the kitchen she opened and shut a few cupboard doors, all the while working her way towards the back door. Then, as quickly as she could, her bare feet soundless on the tile, she unlatched the door, stepped through, and pulled it shut behind her.

She had not been this way before. The back door opened on to a flagstoned patio, the very flagstones on which she had nearly fallen the day she had signalled from the roof. The patio was bordered with earthenware pots of trailing lobelia and nasturtiums, petunias and marigolds, around which a few bees hummed in industrious chorus. Beyond it the grass stretched down the slope towards the river. Sean had mentioned that he had a boat moored there; she'd go and look at it.

Feeling better already, ignoring the faint twinges of guilt for having deceived Baron, who would undoubtedly be blamed for it and of whom she had become very fond despite his jailer role, she strode down the little pathway of beaten grass. More and more of the river was coming into view as she walked; she saw that the path disappeared into a thicket of trees before it reached the shoreline, where she could glimpse a tall mast swaying gently from side to side. Perhaps that was where Sean had gone ... he'd be, to say the least, surprised to see her. At the moment she really didn't care whether the surprise was pleasant or unpleasant.

Her only warning was a single high-pitched bark. She looked back at the house. Baron had just come round the corner and had caught sight of her. He was streaking across the grass towards her, belly low to the ground, ears laid back.

For an instant Caroline panicked, images of being torn limb from limb or dragged bodily back up the slope flitting through her mind. But then her chin snapped up. She was *not* going back to the house. No matter what happened, she was not spending one more day cooped up in her room. Resolutely ignoring the dog's approach, head held high, she stalked down the path.

In a swirl of black and tan Baron overtook her, taking up a stance directly in front of her, his white teeth gleaming. She tried to walk around him. He moved to prevent her. Back the other way. Again the big body planted itself between her and the river. 'Baron,' she ordered, 'get out of my way.'

No altering of the watchful posture, no wavering of the golden eyes. Once again she tried to circumvent him, and this time there came a low, rumbling growl from deep in his chest.

One glance at the river, so tantalisingly near, so totally out of reach, and all because of a dog, and Caroline lost her temper. Hands on her hips, she filled her lungs with air and yelled at the top of her voice, 'Sean Reilly—call off your dog!'

A robin chirped in the trees, and a vagrant breeze

stirred the branches. Ripples washed up on the shore in a gentle, ageless rhythm. Not at all in the mood to appreciate nature's serene beauty, Caroline stood akimbo, her eyes glittering with pure rage. 'Sean!' she yelled again. 'Call Baron!'

'There's no need to shout. I'm right here.'

She whirled, her hair swinging around her face. Although he seemed to have emerged from nowhere, and certainly she had not heard his approach, she saw that there must be a short-cut to the shore down a slope to her right. The very mildness of his reply infuriated her even further. Biting off her words, she repeated, 'Call off your dog!'

'There's a marvellous little word in the English language—it's called please.'

She scowled at him. 'I'm going to walk to the shore. I don't give a damn what Baron does nor do I give a damn what you do—but that's what *I'm* going to do.'

'You really are astonishingly beautiful when you're angry.'

'*Oh!*' Her nails curled into her palm; for the first time in her life she understood how people could throw things at each other. It would give her great satisfaction to be able to fling something at him, to hear a platter shatter against a wall—or against his head, she thought vengefully.

'Baron, come.' The dog got up, loped over to his master, and licked his hand. 'Why don't you come and see the boat?' Sean suggested calmly.

'I'd love to—maybe I could push you both overboard.'

'Nice day for a swim.'

She would not laugh . . . she would not. 'Which way do we go?' she asked tightly.

He grinned at her. 'If I lead the way, promise not to push me down the hill?'

'I won't promise anything.'

He tilted his head to one side, eyes narrowed against

the sun. 'You look as though you'd slit my throat first chance you got.'

'I'm sick to death of being cooped up in that room!' Caroline exploded.

Sean said, a peculiar note in his voice, 'You've lasted much longer than I thought you would.'

'Why don't we go and see your boat,' she replied with no great degree of politeness; the last thing she wanted right now was a nice intellectual discussion of Gabrielle versus Caroline.

Perhaps he felt the same way. 'Follow me.'

The path disappeared into the trees, the quivering leaves of the aspens sprinkling the ground with moving shadows; the robin sounded much closer now. They descended a series of dips and hollows, and then made a final undignified scramble over worn, moss-covered rocks to the shore. The tide was high, so the river lapped almost to their feet. Stepping gingerly over the slippery rocks, Caroline felt the water cool on her bare toes and wriggled them in childlike delight, forgetting Sean and Baron and her own ill-temper. The sun laved her skin with warmth, dancing from ripple to ripple in flashes of light even as the breeze tugged at her hair and the brackish tang of the river filled her nostrils. Throwing back her head, closing her eyes, she inhaled deeply, and all the disquietude of the past few days dropped from her as if it had never been.

Sean looked back over his shoulder, and she smiled at him. 'What a heavenly place!'

He had rolled up the legs of his jeans and tied his canvas sneakers in a loop around his neck. He was wearing a white T-shirt that, while clean, could not be called anything but old, for the sleeves had been torn out and the neckline was frayed; it fitted him like a second skin so that she could see the arc of his ribcage, the flat, taut belly, and the shadow of hair through the worn material. Her eyes dropped, and from the trees the robin called again.

He said roughly, 'The dinghy is over there. We have to row out to the boat.'

Keeping a careful distance between them, Caroline waded towards the dinghy, which was flat-bottomed, looked homemade, and was painted an eye-stopping shade of yellow. 'You wouldn't lose that in the dark,' she commented.

'Yellow is one of my favourite colours. That's why I picked out a yellow shirt for you.'

He was watching her, his eyes lingering on the swell of her breasts under the pale yellow fabric. A blush stained her cheeks, rather spoiling her attempt to sound composed. 'I'm glad you didn't try and match the dinghy.' Wanting to change the subject, she added, 'The canoe over there, is that yours too?'

The canoe, an aluminium one, had been pulled up into the bushes and turned keel up. 'No, that belongs to Ian, the friend who owns the house.'

Sean had been hauling the dinghy off the rocks into the water while he spoke. Seating her in the stern and inserting the oars into the oarlocks, he began rowing with an absent-minded ease that was beautiful to watch, the muscles rippling under his skin in a way that made Caroline shiver with secret pleasure. Skilfully he brought the dinghy alongside the sloop and helped her aboard.

She stood on the deck, looking around her with interest. 'What's her name?'

He answered with faint defensiveness. *'Primrose.'*

Her eyes danced up at him; it seemed far too pretty a name for a boat owned by someone as tough, as virile, and as capable as Sean. 'Oh?'

'I told you I liked yellow.'

'So you did. Take me on the grand tour.'

They went over the boat from bow to stern, Caroline's head whirling with nautical terms. Stays, shrouds, cleats. Pulpit, mainsail, genoa. What she could appreciate was the immaculate cleanliness of the boat, the neatness of the lines, the shine of the railings. Below deck she was fascinated by the tiny cabin, where every inch of space was put to use, and where again tidiness and order prevailed.

'I've never gone sailing,' she remarked. 'It looks like fun.'

'It can be. It can also be hellish uncomfortable. But you're free out there on the open water. Free of all the ordinary restrictions. The winds, the tides, the currents, they're your masters, and you need all your strength and skill to use them to your advantage.'

'So it's the challenge of you against nature.'

'Not against—with.'

She felt the old familiar lift of excitement, and said spontaneously, 'I'd like to try it some time.'

Sean was standing very close to her, his head bent because he was too tall for the cabin. He said abruptly, 'We'd better go back. I'm half-expecting my friends to phone today or tomorrow—the ones who own the house.'

It was an excuse, and she knew it. Turning away so he wouldn't see the hurt in her face, she clambered through the raised hatch and, without waiting to be helped, got back into the dinghy, her eyes glued to the rocks as he rowed ashore. Getting out, she said politely. 'Thank you.'

No answer. Sean hauled the dinghy up on the shale and then led the way up the path back into the woods. Baron had gone ahead. Caroline trailed along behind, absurdly wanting to cry. Ever since she had come here, she had refused to look ahead into the future, for she had no idea where this drama was going to end. Now she found herself wondering how she could ever bear to leave him, yet equally how she could bear to continue being with him. Advance, then retreat; belief, then distrust. He played on her emotions as if she was on a seesaw.

Sean had stopped in the middle of the path, one hand

held back to alert her, but absorbed in her own thoughts, she had not even noticed and walked straight into him. 'Shh,' he murmured. 'Look in the first tree behind this maple. See? It's a Baltimore oriole.'

She edged around him, saw movement among the leaves and a flash of colour. For an instant she saw the bird, its plumage a vibrant mix of black and brilliant orange, as if it had gathered both the depth of night and the fire of the sun into its feathers. Then it was gone and there were only green leaves waving lazily in the breeze.

'There's a pair nesting around here somewhere, but I've never discovered where,' said Sean in a more ordinary voice. 'They're relatively rare. You did see it, didn't you?'

Caroline looked up at him. 'Yes. . . .' Her voice died away, for suddenly there was a look in his eyes that drove everything from her mind but his closeness.

Like a man who cannot help himself, he brought his hands up to cup her face, which was dappled with the shadows of the aspen leaves, her eyes as mysterious as the deep water of the river. He let his mouth drift across her forehead, down the hollowed cheekbone to the soft, trembling mouth.

In that single kiss was all the glory of the sun. His hands moved over her body almost desperately, as if he was trying to re-learn every contour of it all at once, as if there was no time but only raw, unappeasable hunger. And her own need of him leaped to answer his, her lips parting for the dizzying touch of his, her body pressing itself against him.

Somehow they were on the ground, pillowed by the grass and the vivid wildflowers, a canopy of leaves overhead. Then Sean's head blotted out even that. He lowered his weight on her, kissing her hair, her eyes, her throat, until she herself guided him to her mouth.

It was a kiss that seemed to last for ever, and offered

a fusion of two bodies that was its own reward even as it led to an even greater fulfilment. Caroline had never felt so fiercely herself, so aware of her own singing flesh and racing blood; yet the pounding of her own heart was inseparable from Sean's and the heat of her skin from his, and she gloried in both.

Clothes were discarded in awkward, unspoken haste until there was again, after so many days and nights, the hardness of his chest against her soft breasts and the sweetness of his mouth seeking their tips. Over and over again Caroline repeated his name, like the sighing of the wind in the trees, all her longing and pleasure naked in her voice as with hands and mouth he brought her breasts to an aching, swollen fullness.

He slid her shorts from her hips and kicked free of his jeans, throwing himself across her to find her mouth again. The shock ran through her whole body as she felt against her thighs the fierce, driving hardness that was his manhood, all the pride and fire of him, all his unspoken need for her. Deep in her throat she moaned his name as his hands cupped her hips, moving her against him, then drifted, as light and confident as the flight of a bird, to touch between her legs.

Amidst the gathering tumult of her body, there was a fleeting brush of fear. Her eyes dark as night, she murmured against his mouth, 'Sean, I want you—oh, so much. But be gentle with me, won't you? I've never been with a man before. . . .'

She had completely forgotten the existence of Gabrielle, for after all, what had Gabrielle to do with this? Nothing. She had no part in this newfound intimacy. So it was like a physical blow when Sean suddenly raised his head, the passion ebbing from his face like the turning of the tide, his eyes as hard as the stones on the shore. 'I'd forgotten,' he muttered, briefly closing his eyes as if he could not bear to look at her. 'God in heaven, I'd forgotten!'

In her bones she knew what was coming, and knew

herself defenceless against the hurt. 'Forgotten what?' she faltered.

He flung himself off her, reaching for his jeans and without a trace of selfconsciousness pulling them on. Caroline sat up, too frightened to care that she was naked. 'You must tell me——'

He looked down at her, seeing her half in sun, half in shadow. 'I won't make love to you not knowing who you are.'

She had expected nothing different, yet it was like the twisting of a knife in her heart. Scarcely knowing what she was saying, she cried, 'What are we going to *do*?'

'We're not going to do anything,' he said harshly, throwing her her clothes without looking at her.

Along with all her normal defences, her pride seemed to have vanished, too. 'I can't go on like this, Sean, it's too painful. With one hand you pull me close, with the other you push me away. I—I just can't bear it!'

'Put your clothes on,' he said in a clipped voice.

It was the final, fatal twist of the knife blade. She paled. 'You hate me, don't you?' she whispered.

He dropped to his knees beside her, clasping her by the shoulders with a cruel strength she was sure he was not even aware of. 'I don't know what the hell I feel any more,' he snarled. 'Don't you understand that? I'm being torn apart. I want to believe you're as innocent and as free and as beautiful as you seem, every instinct in me screams to believe you. But then my brain intervenes and reminds me how clever Gabrielle is, and how unscrupulous and deceptive, and I'm caught in the middle not knowing what to believe.'

He was shaking her until her teeth rattled. Caroline croaked, 'You're hurting!'

Knowing him as well, it seemed, as she knew herself, she saw the conflict vanish from his face and reason return. As if contact with her was burning his fingers, he let go of her, his features corroded with self-disgust. 'I'm sorry,' he muttered. 'I didn't even know what I was doing.' Standing up, he turned his back on her. 'Get dressed and we'll go back to the house.'

Her fingers would not obey her. On the first attempt she put her shirt on back to front, and then she broke a fingernail in the zipper on her shorts. But finally she was ready. Sean started up the path ahead of her, still not looking at her, and she stumbled along behind, her eyes hot and dry, the beginnings of a headache threatening her temples. It was not until she was alone in her room, the door firmly shut, that she allowed the words to surface. *I have to leave here*, she thought, gazing at her strained features in the mirror in dry-eyed desperation. *Somehow I have to get away. Because I can't stand to stay any longer, loving him as I do.*

CHAPTER EIGHT

THE hurricane hit in the night. At two o'clock Caroline got up and closed her bedroom window, for the curtains were flapping in the wind and rain was blowing in over the floor. It was pitch black outside, a darkness torn by the shriek of the gale and the lash of rain against the glass: a night to be indoors. Shivering a little, she went back to bed, burrowing her head under the covers, for there was something frightening in the storm's impersonal violence.

It took her a long time to get to sleep again, and when she woke next it was daylight. If anything the force of the wind seemed greater, the beat of rain like the insistent drumming of fingers on the windowpane, all seeking to get in, the wind screaming encouragement. The room was filled with grey light; wondering what time it was, she saw that her electric clock was dead, indicating that the power was off. Hardly surprising in such a storm.

About to try and get to sleep again, she suddenly lay still, a frown of concentration on her face. What had she heard, blown on the wind? There it was again . . . a dog barking. Baron.

None of her business. Sean would look after it. She huddled under the quilt, burying her nose in the pillow and resolutely shutting her eyes. Sean was the last person she wanted to see. Today she must try and work out some kind of a plan for escape, and once she was away from here she must learn to forget him. Put him out of her mind as if she had never met him. . . .

A whole chorus of barks this time, and closer, almost as if Baron was right under her window. Caroline found herself sitting up in bed, eyes wide open. For some reason she was sure he had been barking for a long time; it was not the full-throated bay she had grown used to, but almost a yelp, as if he was very tired. She got out of bed, running to the window, but it was useless to even try and see out, for the rain was pouring down the pane in sheets, and she knew better than to raise the sash. Hurriedly pulling on her jeans and the pale yellow T-shirt—which she was beginning to heartily dislike— she went to the door and opened it.

Instantly she was certain that the house was deserted; there was something in the waiting silence underlying the cacophony of the storm that emphasised her solitude. Not stopping to think, for if she had she would never have done it, she hurried across the hall. Sean's door was ajar. When she looked round it, she saw an unmade bed in an empty room.

Her nerves beginning to tighten uncomfortably, she ran downstairs and unlatched the front door, taking a firm grasp on it before she opened it. It was as well she had. The wind was like a living thing, shoving the door rudely inwards so that she staggered, her bare feet seeking a purchase on the floor.

She did not need to call, for with the opening door came Baron. Using all her strength, Caroline pushed it shut and slipped the chain in place. Baron was whimpering. He was also soaking wet, his fur plastered to his body so that he looked almost emaciated. He nudged at her with his massive head, nearly knocking her off balance.

'What is it? Where's Sean?'

He loped across the hall, leaving a wet trail behind him, looking back over his shoulder at her. The message was unmistakable. Trying to avoid stepping where he had been, Caroline followed him into the kitchen and through to the back door. There the dog sat down, raised his head to the ceiling, and gave a high-pitched howl that sent shivers up her spine.

Wishing he could talk, she said helplessly, 'Something's wrong, isn't it? Is Sean outside?'

Another spine-tingling howl. Trying to forget a movie she had seen as a young girl where the faithful dog had howled pitifully over its master's grave to great dramatic effect, she grabbed a jacket of Sean's from one of the hooks by the back door, catching from it an elusive trace of his aftershave, then raced upstairs to get her socks and sneakers. The old grandfather clock in the corner of the kitchen said nine-thirty; it was the storm that made everything seem so dark.

Baron was whimpering again. Caroline laced up her sneakers with fingers that were slightly unsteady and did up the zipper on the jacket, putting the hood over her hair and pulling the drawstring tight. 'Let's go,' she said to the dog; he was already standing with his nose pressed to the door.

The patio was sheltered by the angle of the house. Someone, presumably Sean, had moved the flowerpots into the corner. Baron ran across the flagstones to the path that led down the hill, the wind flattening his ears to his head as he emerged into the open. For a moment Caroline hesitated, awed by the power of the storm. Black-edged clouds scudded across the sky. The trees had been whipped into a frenzy, bending before the gale; even as she watched, a branch was torn from an old elm and tangled itself in the thrashing limbs of a tall pine. Through the sheets of rain she could not distinguish *Primrose*'s mast, although she could see the driven waves on the river, white-capped with spume blown from the crests.

Baron yelped imperatively, and she dragged herself back to the matter at hand. Bracing herself, she stepped out into the open.

Staggering, eyes narrowed against the downpour, she followed Baron down the hill. Within minutes her feet were wet through, for the grass was saturated, the daisies and toadflax flattened to the ground; her jeans were stuck to her legs and the jacket had begun to leak through the seams. But these were minor inconveniences, because she knew now that Sean was in some kind of trouble, and the closer they got to the river, the more afraid she became.

The trees offered little or no shelter, the branches slapping at her as she passed, broken twigs littering the path. She could hear the river now, a rhythmic splash of waves on the rocks and a rattle of stones as the waves receded. Scrambling down the last slope, she clung to the bushes, for the tide was higher than yesterday, lapping at the very base of the hillside. Fighting for breath, she looked over at *Primrose*.

The sloop was tugging at her moorings, bucking the waves with the bright yellow dinghy fastened to her stern. There was no sign of Sean.

For a moment Caroline stood paralysed. He must be on board the sloop if the dinghy was there; but unless something had happened to him, why would he remain on board? And how was she to get out there to find out?

Then she remembered the canoe. It had been hauled further into the bushes so its bow was part way up the slope. She righted it, untying the hawser and removing the paddles from the thwarts. 'Stay, Baron,' she called to the drenched dog, and then without giving herself time to think launched the canoe, sitting nearly amidships and paddling as hard as she could; if she broached in these waves, she would quite literally be sunk, she thought with grim humour.

It took the best part of fifteen minutes to cover the relatively short distance to the sloop. Tying the canoe to the dinghy, she clambered over it to get aboard *Primrose*'s stern.

She saw Sean immediately. He was crumpled in a heap in the cockpit, lying in a puddle of water that sloshed back and forth with the rocking of the boat. His clothing was soaked, clinging to his skin while his hair was a cluster of wet curls.

Caroline dropped to her knees beside him, turning his head so that she could see his face. His cheek was streaked with blood from an ugly laceration which ran from his forehead into his hair and which was surrounded by a swollen, purple bruise. His eyes were closed, his face deathly pale. Frantically she sought for the pulse in his wrist, almost crying with relief as she felt it under her fingertips. She ran her hands over his arms and legs, making reasonably sure that nothing was broken. Then she sat back on her heels, wondering what on earth she was going to do, the thoughts chasing each other through her head.

There was no telephone at the house; Sean himself had made sure of that. She would have to drive at least five miles in a totally unfamiliar car to get help, with no guarantee that a tree had not fallen across the track through the woods. Sean was soaked to the skin, his face and hands cold to the touch. She had no idea how long ago he had hurt himself; Baron could have been barking at her window for some time before she had heard him. She could get Sean into the cabin, where at least he would be out of the rain. But there was no bedding on board, no dry clothes, no way of heating the cabin.

There was only one alternative. Somehow she had to get him up to the house.

A sudden squall lashed the boat, raindrops bounding on the deck and petting her face and hair, and her heart quailed. It was an impossible task—she'd never manage it. She'd have to wait until Sean recovered consciousness and could help himself.

This time when she put her fingers on his wrist it seemed to her in her overwrought state that the pulse was weaker. Her mouth tightened and an expression settled on her face that her ski coach would have recognised: it came from her early days in skiing, when perhaps she was fifteenth in a field of twenty and was determined to make the top five. Resolution, concentration, a drawing on resources she scarcely knew she possessed.

Putting her hands under Sean's armpits, she dragged him round to the stern, taking as little of his weight as she could. Thank God he had an outboard motor, so there was a well in the transom—it gave her at least a fighting chance to get him in the dinghy.

Afterwards, when Caroline looked back on the whole experience, the first ten minutes were the worst, for both the sloop and the dinghy were at the mercy of wind and waves, and Sean was a dead weight. But somehow, sliding him inch by inch, she managed it, although at the last, when he thudded across the thwarts of the dinghy, she was terrified they were going to swamp. She pulled him as low in the boat as she could, slipped the knot on the hawser, and began to row, the canoe bobbing in their wake.

The wind was with her; the danger was that the dinghy be swamped at the stern. Pull, pull, pull . . . and then the bow scraped on the rocks. Jumping out, she hauled the boat up on the shore as far as she could.

She thought Baron's tail would wag right off; as it was, it sent showers of spray into the air. He sniffed at Sean's face, whining in his throat, and Caroline said, unashamedly pleased to have his company, 'You're going to have to help, old boy. We've got to get him up to the house.'

She half dragged, half rolled Sean out of the dinghy, his limp body sprawling on the rocks, and once again she was assailed by sheer terror. That she wouldn't be able to get him up to the house . . . that he would die. Talking to the dog as if he could understand every word, she said, her voice quivering in spite of herself, 'You grab his jacket on that side and pull, and I'll take this side.'

Sean had once told her that Baron had been police-trained; she now realised with a surge of thankfulness that made her knees weak that part of that training must have been pulling people to safety, perhaps from fires, perhaps from damaged buildings. It didn't matter . . . all that mattered was that as they inched their way across the shingle, the water sucking at Sean's feet and legs, Baron was taking a fair share of the weight.

The first slope was the most difficult, for it was the steepest and very rocky. Once Caroline slipped, tearing her jacket and scraping her elbow, and, more important, losing a couple of feet of the precious ground they had gained. Her muscles aching with the strain, her legs braced against the angle of the slope, she took a new hold on Sean's shoulder and pulled until she thought her arms would break. Foot by foot she and the dog dragged their inanimate burden up the hill.

The path was more level in the woods so that it seemed almost easy in comparison. But by the time they reached the open field below the house, Caroline knew her stamina was running out. For a moment she dropped down on the grass, letting her head fall forward on her knees, her breath heaving in her lungs, her limbs trembling from the effort. Baron pushed his cold wet nose against her face and she flung an arm over him, desperately trying to recoup her strength.

She stayed there for nearly five minutes, almost in a daze. Then, only because there was no alternative, she shoved herself upright and bent to take Sean by the shoulder again. Trying to focus on anything but the debilitating exhaustion of her body, she tried counting the clumps of grass and the broken-stemmed daisies, and then her own steps. Ten, eleven, twelve . . . twenty-four, twenty-five, twenty-six. Then underfoot the grass was suddenly shorter and neatly mowed, and with a sob of relief she knew they were nearly there.

The last stretch seemed to go on for ever. But, like all nightmares, it had to end. They reached the flagstones, where her feet could get a better purchase, and finally she opened the back door, tugging Sean bodily over the steps, knowing she must be bruising his back but helpless to prevent it. When he was lying flat on the tiled floor, she closed the door, leaning against it with her eyes closed. None of her training, certainly none of her races, had ever left her as tired as she was now.

Baron flopped down on the floor, nose on his paws, his flanks heaving. She whispered shakily, 'Good dog! I could never have done it alone,' and was rewarded by a wet slap of his tail which did nothing for the cleanliness of the floor.

Slowly she straightened. *I can't just stand here*, she thought dully. *There are things to be done.*

Moving like an old woman, she took off her jacket and unlaced her sneakers, leaving them in a heap by the door, before going upstairs. In her room she pulled the duvet from the closet and the quilt from the bed, taking a couple of pillows as well as a heap of clean towels from the bathroom. She laid the quilt and pillows on the chesterfield and went back into the kitchen.

Sean was lying where she had left him. Trying to remember her lessons on first aid, Caroline knelt beside him, opening one eye. His lids twitched, and then his head moved. He muttered something incomprehensible before lapsing into stillness again.

Her eyes swimming with tears of sheer relief, she found the strength to pull him across the hall into the living room and lever him up on the chesterfield. Moving as quickly as she could, she took off his wet clothes and dried him with the towels, her heart aching with compassion for his helplessness. He was stirring again. Quickly she tucked the folds of the duvet around him, put the kettle on for hot water bottles, and laid a fire.

Within half an hour the living room was deliciously warm, the flames leaping up the chimney. Baron had stretched himself out by the hearth, his steaming fur exuding a very strong odour of dog. Caroline didn't care: he had earned it.

She had bathed Sean's forehead, and already his hands and feet were warmer, a bit of colour creeping into his cheeks. He had opened his eyes two or three times, blinking against the light; sensing his pain and confusion, she made no attempt to talk to him.

She herself was still in her wet clothes, for there had been more important things to deal with than that. But now, after checking that Sean was resting comfortably and that the screen was safely in front of the fire, she went upstairs again. A quick shower did wonders for her morale as well as her cleanliness, although it made the scrape on her elbow sting; wrapping herself in a towel, she padded to Sean's room to find something to wear. She was definitely not going to wear the navy nightdress at this hour of the day.

It seemed a very intimate thing to go into his room and open the latticed cupboard door; his clothes, most of which she recognised, were hanging together at the near end of the rail. She went through them until she came to a burgundy robe of lightweight wool edged with silk. It would be too big, but it would cover her and be warm until she could get her jeans and shirt washed and dried. Slipping it on, she belted it tightly around her waist and rolled up the cuffs, giggling at her reflection in the mirror, too taken by the robe's masculine proportions to notice how its deep, glowing hue gave her skin a pearly sheen, or how its very size emphasised the fragility of her throat and wrists.

Gathering all the wet clothes, she went downstairs again and dumped them by the washer—useless, with the power still off. Pushing open the living room door, she slipped inside.

'Who's there?'

His voice had only a fraction of its normal resonance, but it was still Sean's voice. Caroline hurried over to the chesterfield, dropping to her knees beside it so that her face was on a level with his, her expression mirroring her profound relief. His eyes were open, although he was frowning as if he was having difficulty focussing them. 'I—what am I doing here?' he muttered.

'You had an accident on the boat and knocked yourself out.'

'On the boat? But——'

She rested her palm gently on his cheek, her eyes brilliant with tears. 'Hush—don't worry about it now. It's enough that you're all right.' Knowing she was going to cry and that there was absolutely nothing she could do to prevent it, she buried her head in the duvet somewhere in the vicinity of his shoulder, her own shoulders shaking.

Awkwardly Sean freed his arm from the covers and put it around her, rubbing the nape of her neck. 'Your hair's wet,' he said, puzzled.

'It's raining,' she hiccupped. 'And that's the understatement of the year!'

'I—I don't understand. . . .' His hand slid limply down her back, his breathing deepening. She looked up, rubbing at her eyes, knowing with another rush of gratitude that he was asleep again, a more natural sleep this time. Tucking his arm under the duvet, she went to dry her hair by the fire, remembering another day when a man had dried her hair in the sun. . . .

The minutes and hours passed slowly. Outside, the gale rattled the window and the rain swept in curtains across the field, but inside the house was warm and cosy. Caroline made a trip to the basement for more wood, made herself lunch on the little wood stove in the kitchen, and then curled up in the armchair by the fire with a book. Twice Sean had roused, but he was plainly still confused with no clear idea of what had happened, and each time he had fallen asleep again. She herself, lulled by the warmth and overtired from all her exertions, soon gave up any pretence of reading. The book slipped to the floor, her lashes closed, and her head fell back.

Someone was calling her name. *Caroline*, they were saying. *Caroline.* . . .

Wincing from a crick in her neck, Caroline opened her eyes. On the chesterfield Sean was half sitting up, resting his weight on one elbow, his shoulders and chest bare. It was he who had been calling her, she thought dazedly, grimacing as she straightened, for her whole body had been uncomfortably twisted in the chair. 'You called me Caroline,' she blurted.

'You didn't stir when I called you Gabrielle.'

There was something in his eyes she couldn't decipher. She got up, putting a couple of logs on the fire, watching the sparks shower up the chimney as if she had never seen anything quite so fascinating in her life before. From behind her Sean said, 'Come here.'

She turned to face him, belatedly realising that the neckline of the robe had gaped open while she slept; pulling the edges together, she belted it more tightly, her cheeks tinged with pink. 'What do you want?'

He patted the duvet. 'Come and sit down.'

Almost reluctantly she did as he asked. 'You look a lot better,' she ventured. 'Can I get you anything?'

His smile was heart-stoppingly familiar. 'On a very practical level, I need to go to the bathroom. I don't seem to have any clothes on, and you're wearing my robe.'

'All your clothes were wet,' Caroline mumbled, picking at the duvet with her fingernails.

With one finger he raised her chin. 'You look much better in it than I do. But would you mind finding me something to wear? I think if you look in the closet near the back you'll find an old blue robe of Ian's—I'm sure he wouldn't mind if I borrowed it. And then when I come back downstairs, I want you to tell me what happened. I've got one hell of a sore head!'

She took refuge in impudence. 'It's a good thing you've got a thick skull! I'll be right back.'

She soon found the garment he was referring to, ran back downstairs with it and busied herself poking at the fire while he put it on. 'You can look now,' he said dryly. 'I'm perfectly decent.'

She turned to find him standing at the far end of the chesterfield, leaning against the wall with one hand; he was very pale, his eyes sunk in his head. 'Are you all right?' she asked sharply.

'No. I'm as weak as a day-old kitten and my legs won't hold me up. Can you give me a hand?'

He put his arm heavily on her shoulders, finding every one of her sore muscles. With an arm about his waist, she steadied him as best she could out in the hall and up the stairs. By the time they reached the bathroom door he was sweating, lines of pain scoring his cheeks. 'I'll wait up here,' she said in as ordinary a tone of voice as she could manage.

'Thanks.'

She did some unnecessary tidying in her room while she was waiting, wondering if she shouldn't get dressed in Gabrielle's culottes, yet strangely reluctant to do so. Because she didn't want to remind Sean of Gabrielle? Or because she liked wearing his robe, catching from it the elusive scent of his body, a clean, male fragrance that pleased her?

It seemed to take him a very long time. When he finally emerged, he looked even worse than he had before. He smiled at her ruefully. 'Sorry to take so long. I've just lost what feels like every meal I've eaten in the last week.'

'That's a horrible feeling, isn't it?' she commiserated. 'Are you ready to do downstairs?'

'Yeah.'

They made it down the stairs, Sean obviously trying not to rest too much of his weight on her yet unable to wholly support himself. She helped him sit down again on the chesterfield, flinching as her sore elbow hit the armrest. 'Did I hurt you?' he demanded.

'I scraped my arm on the rocks.'

'Let me see.'

'It's really nothing——'

He took her arm, pushing the sleeve back and exposing the grazed skin. 'It looks clean, although maybe you should put some antiseptic on it. How did you do it?'

'Lie down first,' Caroline said anxiously, for he looked terrible.

It was a measure of his weakness that without protest he did as he was told. 'Sit down beside me,' he murmured; somehow he had retained hold of her hand. She found herself looking at the long lean fingers encircling her own much smaller ones, and feeling simple happiness suffuse her whole being. Not for anything in the world would she have been anywhere but where she was.

Trying not to make too much of it, she told how she had woken to Baron's barking and followed him to the shore, and how the two of them had brought Sean up to the house. 'Maybe I should have taken you straight to the doctor, but I was afraid to drive the car through the woods,' she finished lamely.

He said very carefully, 'You mean you got me off the sloop into the dinghy, then from the beach all the way up here?'

'Baron helped—I couldn't have done it alone.' There was an expression in his face she had never seen before, and unaccountably she blushed. 'What choice did I have, Sean? There was no dry clothing or heat on the boat, and no telephone at the house to call for help.'

'That's really being hoist with my own petard, isn't it? Look at me—why didn't you just leave me there and take off? It was a perfect chance.'

'I couldn't have done that,' she said, shaken. 'You might have died.'

'You could have phoned the police in town and told them to go and get me.'

'It never even occurred to me to leave you there. If you'd been in my place, you wouldn't have, would you?'

Insensibly his face relaxed. 'Your syntax is a bit muddled, but no, I don't suppose I would. You did a very brave and difficult thing—thank you, Caro.'

He must have seen the joy that flared in her eyes at his use of her nickname. 'It wasn't particularly brave,' she disclaimed. 'But you're heavy enough that it was certainly difficult!'

'*I* think it was brave. You're the one who got me to shore, after all.' He gave her hand a tug. 'Come and lie down beside me for a while. I want to hold on to you.'

'I don't think——'

'You don't have to worry, I'm in no state to be any threat to your virtue. Stop arguing.'

She didn't want to argue, that was the trouble. She wanted to do exactly as he had asked. Obediently she slid under the covers. He put his arms around her so that her back was pulled against his chest and her head tucked under his chin; her whole body quivered as one hand curved round her belly, the other resting on her breast. But then he lay still, and gradually she relaxed, allowing herself to enjoy the warmth and intimacy of an embrace that surely sprang from more than gratitude. Against her ear he murmured, 'Are you comfortable?'

She nodded. 'You feel nice.'

'So do you.' Against her shoulder blade she could feel the beating of his heart; she had never before felt so utterly secure. She sensed when he fell asleep, and her own lashes drifted to her cheeks. She didn't want to leave him, and she was very tired. It wouldn't hurt if she closed her eyes just for a few minutes.

But when she next opened them, it was dark. The fire had died down, and the room was cold. Beside her Sean slept peacefully, one arm still resting on her hip. The next thing that struck her was the silence: she could even hear the ticking of the grandfather clock in the kitchen. There was no howling of the wind or beat of rain against the windowpanes. The storm had ended.

With exquisite care so as not to disturb Sean, she lifted his arm from her hip, edged herself off the chesterfield, and went over to the fireplace. It was impossible, she soon found, to bank up a fire that was nearly gone out and remain absolutely quiet. The screen squeaked on its tracks. Paper had to be crumpled into tight balls, kindling laid across the paper and then logs put on top, all of which seemed to make an inordinate amount of noise, Baron's tail on the floor providing the counterpoint.

The paper caught fire from the coals and the kindling began to spit and crackle. She closed the screen again, and heard Sean say drowsily, 'It needs oiling.'

The fire was catching beautifully. The light dancing over her features, Caroline said, 'I was trying to be quiet, I didn't want to waken you.'

He yawned, 'You haven't, really. Come back to bed.'

She had been walking back to the chesterfield, but that last little phrase stopped her dead. It sounded so ordinary, yet so intimate: the kind of thing he would say very naturally were they married. *I'd like to marry him and share his bed.* 'I'd better sleep upstairs,' she said weakly.

'Don't be silly. It'll be cold up there.' Another yawn. 'Anyway, I've got half your bedding, haven't I?'

True enough. Trying to delay the inevitable, she asked, 'How are you feeling?'

'Lightheaded,' he answered succinctly. 'Come and lie down.'

Wondering if she was being an absolute fool, yet knowing it was exactly what she wanted to do, she lifted the corner of the duvet and crept in beside him. Had it truly been a bed, she could have kept her distance. But it was not; of necessity they had to lie close together.

Just as he had the last time, he pulled her against him, curving his arms around her, making a tiny sound of contentment that touched her as a flood of elaborate endearments might not have.

She lay very still, aware of him in every nerve she possessed, her eyes wide open. The leaping flames were reflected on the walls and the ceiling, without pattern or rhythm, full of a wild energy. The fire was tamed now, safely enclosed. But how quickly it could flare into danger and destruction. . . .

She felt his hand move against her breast and her heart leaped in response, as fiercely and wildly as the flames in the hearth. Then his fingers moved the silk-edged fabric out of the way, finding the soft swell of her flesh under it and caressing it with infinite gentleness.

Time itself was suspended. There was nothing in the world but the touch of his fingers bringing her sheer delight. But it was a pleasure that bordered on pain for, though sweet in itself, it brought with it an insistent demand for more, an ache of desire that spread through her whole body, overpowering common sense and restraint and banishing them as if they did not exist.

She knew he was aroused; in the close confines of their embrace it was impossible not to know. She should leave, she knew that, too. Fight back her deep, instinctive need of him. Leave him and go to her own bed. Gathering every scrap of her resolution she tried to move away.

But Sean totally misinterpreted her. With surprising strength he turned her in his arms so that she faced him, and the robe gaped open, exposing her shoulders and breasts to his view. For a moment he simply held her, his eyes lingering on the swollen nipples and the valley between them, drinking in their beauty. Then he lowered his head, letting his lips and tongue touch where his eyes had been.

Shamelessly Caroline held him close, her fingers stroking his thick, silky hair, her eyes closed as she abandoned herself to his touch. He must have felt her surrender in the tightness of her nipples, in the frantic beat of her heart under his palm. Yet still he persisted until she was whimpering deep in her throat, a wordless, urgent plea for something more.

Only then did he raise his head, seizing her mouth in his. Her hands kneaded his neck and dug into the hard planes of his back, exulting in the supple flow of muscle. But then he broke free of her, his face only inches from hers as his gaze devoured the sensual, swollen lips, the flushed cheeks and dazzled velvety eyes. Very deliberately he took off his own gown, and equally slowly eased her arms from hers, unbelting it to reveal the slender lines of waist and hip and thigh.

When his eyes came back to her face, she met them bravely, the pulse racing in her throat, her colour heightened, for with one hand he was tracing the rise of her breast, the smooth, flat belly, the hardness of hipbone and the slim length of thigh. And then, as she had known it must, it moved to the place where she had never been touched by a man before.

She arched in instinctive response, his hand the centre of the universe. Lost to everything but drives as old as time that were enveloping her in their primitive rhythms, certainly lost to any pain, Caroline was ready for his ultimate invasion of her, welcoming the thrust of his manhood as it gathered all the rhythms and drove them inexorably towards their crashing climax, losing herself in him as he in her. There were no separate bodies, no Sean and Caroline; only a union that was the very heart of the flame, indescribable, ephemeral, yet more real than anything she had ever known. . . .

It could not last for ever. The glory slowly faded, leaving herself, a woman, lying supine under Sean, a man. But he had not withdrawn from her. She put her arms around him, feeling the long curve of his spine and the sweat slippery on his back, exulting in his weight, wanting to hold him this close to her and never let him go. And strangely she found herself being glad that she had never indulged in any of the casual affairs of the skiing crowd, that she had never gone to bed with anyone simply for the sake of losing her virginity or satisfying her curiosity. For it would not have been like this, so total, so all-encompassing, so right . . . so much an expression of love.

Sean's head had dropped to her shoulder. In faint alarm she realised his forehead was burning hot. She touched it lightly with her fingertips; it too was wet with sweat. 'Are you all right?' she whispered.

Laughter rumbled in his chest. 'You've finished me off, woman! I'm done for.'

'Sean——'

He nuzzled his lips into her neck. 'Hush, I'm fine. That was beautiful . . . I've been wanting to make love to you for days.' He kissed her throat, a kiss without passion, and murmured, 'Am I too heavy?'

'No. I like it.'

It was the simple truth: she did. But as his body relaxed on hers in sleep, his breath fanning her skin, she was left with a sensation she could only describe as loneliness. How could she feel lonely with Sean lying so close to her, or estranged from him with the memory of their lovemaking still vivid and alive?

Because, the answer clicked into her brain, *he never called me by name. Not Caro, or Caroline—or Gabrielle. Nothing.*

So what did that mean? That she had simply been available, a woman he found exciting and desirable no matter what her identity? She didn't want to think that. Oh God, she didn't! But more and more it began to seem the logical explanation.

Nonsense, she argued back. A virgin she might have been, but not so innocent or ignorant as not to have realised that Sean had made love to her with care and concern for her needs. He had not just taken her and used her; he had given her pleasure beyond her wildest dreams. He *must* care for her. Which meant he had made love to Caroline, the woman who had rescued him in the storm and whose courage he admired. So had his motive perhaps been gratitude?

Back and forth she went, from one alternative to the other. But none of her arguments could alter the inescapable fact that during the most intimate act of all between man and woman, Sean had not called her by name. In a very real sense she had been made love to; she had only to feel the hardness of his chest and the weight of his thighs on hers to know that. But in another sense she was untouched. More alone than she had ever been. And all because of an earth-shattering closeness that had been nothing but a mirage. . . .

Eventually she must have fallen asleep. It was Sean who woke her, his voice dragging her from the clutch of a nightmare in which she had been hauling him up a cliff, step by painful step, only to find at the top that he was faceless. Without identity. Not Sean at all.

Struggling to free herself from the terror of this vision, Caroline opened her eyes, blinking against the sunlight streaming in the window.

'What have you done to him?'

A rough hand had grabbed her shoulder, pulling her away from the world outside the window, a world of sparkling, rain-wet grass and golden sun. Fingers were digging into her skin with ugly strength, twisting her round to confront an angry, black-haired man; she stared at him blankly. He had a face. It was Sean. But why was she naked? And what was she doing here?

He was shaking her, his features a rictus of mingled frustration and fury. 'Martin—where is he?'

Her tongue felt thick and awkward. Her brain wouldn't obey her. And suddenly she was terrified. The man she had rescued had turned into a monster, eyes crazed with hatred. Sweat beaded his forehead where his hair clung damply, while he had patches of hectic colour high on his cheekbones. She put her palms against his chest and shoved backwards with all her strength. 'Let go!'

But he was far too strong; she might as well have saved herself the effort. Dazedly she saw him fight for control, his breath rasping in her throat. 'I want to know what you've done to Martin, Gabrielle,' he said more reasonably. 'You're the one who saw him last. He loves you. Where is he?'

It was a continuation of the nightmare, all the more horrifying because she was awake. She croaked, 'I'm not Gabrielle——'

'Of course you are—who else would you be?' Then something seemed to strike him. The fury faded from his eyes, to be replaced by consternation as he looked down at their two naked bodies. Horrified, he whispered, 'What have I done? What in God's name have I done?'

With vicious strength he thrust her away, grabbing the old blue robe and pulling it on as he staggered to his feet. Dumbly Caroline watched him stumble to the door, and heard his footsteps heavy on the stairs. Then a door slammed, and there was silence. Burying her face in the pillow, she wept.

CHAPTER NINE

When Caroline finally sat up, huddling the burgundy robe around her, for she felt very cold, the beams of light had moved across the carpet. The pillow was soaking wet. She rarely cried, but on the few occasions when she had, it had brought relief from whatever had been troubling her. Not now. Like the twist of a knife she could recall in every detail the hatred in Sean's eyes as he called her Gabrielle, the horror when he realised he had made love to her ... to the woman who had betrayed his brother, the woman he despised.

She would not cry again. She wouldn't. She bit her lip, fighting back the useless tears. It was over, she thought numbly. She loved a man who was incapable of seeing her as herself, and who would therefore never be able to love her in return. He had brought her great happiness; but now she was paying the price for it in a misery as profound as the happiness had been. She must leave here and never come back, and maybe, somehow, over time, she would forget him. Briefly she closed her eyes, remembering the cataclysmic glory of their union, knowing it would be impossible to forget.

She got up, leaving the disarranged covers without a backward glance, already steeling heart and mind against the treachery of memory. In her room she dressed slowly in Gabrielle's clothes. She had arrived in them; she would leave in them. And she would take nothing that Sean had bought for her.

Sandals dangling from her hand, she went back into the hall. The bathroom door was wide open. Quickly she went in, dabbling her tear-swollen face with cold water as quietly as she could. She was drying herself when she realised that Sean's bedroom door had been tight shut. So that was the door he had slammed, and presumably that's where he was.

It doesn't matter where he is. You've just got to get out of here.

I can't leave here if he's ill.

You'd better leave. He hates you, doesn't he?

Stealthily she crept towards his room and with infinite care turned the knob, opened the door, and peered inside, her heart beating so loudly she was afraid it alone would waken him. She saw him immediately, sprawled face down across the bed, his back rising and falling steadily with his breathing.

All the love she bore for him urged her to at least pull some covers over him. But she couldn't, she knew she couldn't. The risk was too great that he might waken. Her nails digging into her palm, she turned away

Near the door there was a teak bureau. It was a plain, austerely designed piece of furniture with a beautifully shaped pewter vase resting on it, both very much to her taste. But there were two other objects on the bureau: a man's wallet and a set of car keys.

Caroline stared at them, scarcely even breathing. She had to leave here, she knew that. And the logical way to leave was by car. Sean's car.

He stirred on the bed, muttering something under his breath, and she froze into stillness, her throat tight with anxiety. But he did not wake up; he could have no idea she was standing there. Frantically she tried to cudgel her thoughts into some sort of order. She could take his car as far as the village, leave it parked on the street in a conspicuous place with the keys locked inside, and take the bus or the train to Halifax. But to do that she would need money.

Feeling like a thief, hating herself for what she was doing, she picked up the keys and the wallet and left the room, pulling the door shut behind her. She was at the head of the stairs when she heard the car.

A car? she thought in bewilderment. It couldn't be. Who would be coming here?

She ran quickly down the stairs so she could look out of one of the front windows, but before she reached them she heard, unmistakably, two doors slam and the sound of voices, a man's and a woman's, with Baron barking in the background. Hurriedly she thrust the keys and wallet into her purse and pulled on her sandals.

There was a light tap at the front door. Then a key turned in the lock and the door was pushed open, the man holding it for the woman who stepped confidently into the hall as if she had every right to be there. She was saying in a pleasant, light voice, 'I wonder where Sean is,' when she saw Caroline. 'Oh! Who are you?' she asked disingenuously.

Feeling as though she had been thrust on to a stage with no idea of what the play was about or what her lines were, Caroline answered, somewhat less than truthfully, 'I—I'm a friend of Sean's. And you?'

'He must have told you about us—this is our house.'

Caroline fought for composure. 'I see. I'm afraid he didn't tell me your names.'

The man spoke. 'Ian and Joan Somers. Hope we haven't disturbed you, barging in like this.' He was chunky and pleasant-faced, his curly brown hair disordered by the wind, his blue eyes friendly and without guile. His wife was taller than he, an ash-blonde with one of those haircuts that cost a great deal of money, her manner cooler and more contained. Both, Caroline would guess, were in their late thirties; both were wearing the kind of deceptively casual sports clothes that no doubt bore the labels of a famous designer.

'I'm Caroline Travers,' she said politely. 'How do you do? Was Sean expecting you back so soon? He didn't mention it to me.'

'We're not due back for another two weeks,' Ian Somers said easily. 'But we came into Bedford Basin because of the storm warnings, tried to phone and got alarmed because the phone had been disconnected, and decided to run up and check that everything was okay.'

'Where is Sean?' Joan Somers asked, with just the slightest touch of suspicion in her question.

Caroline's brain had been racing while they were talking. Deciding on a discreet mixture of fact and fiction, she looked straight at the other woman. 'He's been ill. There was an accident on the boat, and now he's got a fever. I was about to take his car and run into town to find a doctor when you arrived.'

'Is he upstairs?' Ian asked.

'Yes. I just looked in on him and he's sleeping right now. He had a—a very restless night, maybe it would be as well not to disturb him.' A delicate flush touched her cheeks.

'Of course not,' Ian replied. 'Look, why don't we put the coffee pot on? Then maybe you'd like me to go into town with you. Dr Richards would be the best one to see, wouldn't he, hon?'

'Yes. I'll write down his number. What *is* the matter with the phone, by the way?'

Again Caroline stuck as closely to the truth as possible. 'I think Sean did it on purpose—wanted to get away from it all, I guess.' She smiled blandly at Joan, not at all sure that she liked her. 'It's Dr Richards, is it? I don't think I'll wait for a coffee, if you don't mind, I'd rather get a prescription as soon as possible. And I'll go by myself, that's no problem. Mr Somers, would you mind letting Baron in the back door while I go out the front? I don't want him to follow me.'

'Sure thing. We'll wait here until you get back.'

She smiled impartially at both of them. 'Great! You couldn't have timed it better, I was worried about leaving Sean alone. I'll see you later.'

'I'll get the dog in right now before you go out,' Ian offered. 'Drive carefully—the road's not in great shape after all the rain.'

'I will.' Itching to be gone, praying her impatience

didn't show, Caroline kept the smile pasted on her lips as he went through to the kitchen.

'Have you known Sean long?' Joan Somers asked bluntly.

'It seems like a long time.' Let her interpret that as she may. 'I must go. Goodbye.'

She stepped out of the door and ran across the grass to the carport, terrified that at the last minute something would happen to prevent her departure. Sean would wake up. Or she wouldn't be able to start the Porsche. But when she turned the key, the engine started as sweetly as she could have wished and the gear lever shifted smoothly into reverse. Every nerve on edge, momentarily expecting to see Ian Somers running across the grass yelling, 'Stop, thief!', she turned around on the gravel track and slipped into first. The tyres spun as she put too much pressure on the accelerator, and a shower of stones shot out behind her. Cautiously she eased her foot off the pedal and drove away up the hill, keeping an anxious eye on the rear-view mirror. Nobody in sight, no sign that the Somers suspected anything was wrong. Second gear. The house disappeared as the track reached the trees, and she let out her breath in a sigh of relief. Her only worry now was that Ian Somers might come after her. All she could do was drive as fast as possible and hope Sean would stay asleep until she was well on her way to Halifax.

Everything seemed to go in her favour. Once she was a little more accustomed to the gear shift, the Porsche was a joy to drive: her major difficulty was staying under the speed limit. She parked on the main street directly in front of the police station, knowing with a touch of malice that Sean would appreciate that. Extracting a twenty-dollar bill from his wallet, she scribbled on a slip of paper, 'I'll pay you back as soon as possible,' purposely leaving it unsigned and inserting it between the remaining bills. Then she tucked wallet and keys under the seat, and locked the car.

At the terminal she found that the Halifax bus was due in half an hour, so her timing couldn't have been better. She bought a ticket and sat at the very back of the waiting room with her face behind a newspaper, mechanically turning the pages every so often as if she was indeed reading it. The bus was ten minutes late, each minute dragging like an hour, for momentarily Caroline was expecting Sean or Ian to burst into the depot and haul her bodily back to the house or, worse, to the police station. Theft of a car and a twenty-dollar bill. Impersonating another woman who happened to be a drug dealer. The village police would have fun with that. Especially if she in turn accused Sean of kidnapping.

The big blue and white bus drew up outside in a cloud of exhaust fumes. Lowering the paper, Caroline took a quick look around and hurried on board, giving up her ticket and sitting near the back by the window. It was not untl they had roared away from the bus terminal and were accelerating down the highway that she began to relax. She had done it! She was on her way home.

Briefly she amused herself by picturing the scene she had left behind her. Joan and Ian Somers patiently waiting for her return, Sean waking up and finding them there, hearing from them how she had taken his car from under their noses, discovering that his wallet was gone as well. What would he tell them? One thing was certain—he wouldn't tell them the truth.

Let him explain away the untidy living room and the two pillows on the chesterfield, her lack of luggage, her mysterious disappearance, she thought unkindly. It would serve him right!

This mood of rare vindictiveness lasted for about twenty miles before, inexorably, depression began to seep in to take its place. Sure, she had managed her escape just beautifully. But what did it mean? It meant she had cut herself off from all contact with Sean. She had no idea of his permanent address, nor did he know hers. It was entirely possible that she might never see him again. *Never* . . . the word was like a lead weight settling on her heart. With agonising clarity she remembered their lovemaking in all its mingled tenderness and fierce demands, its intimacy and startling joy . . . *never again.* How would she bear it?

She stared out of the window, fighting back tears of desolation, trying to concentrate on the serene beauty of the passing landscape, where the Annapolis River meandered lazily through the flat green fields against the timeworn bulk of North Mountain. The meadows were punctuated by weathered barns, herds of Holsteins and Guernsey cattle, and groves of stately elms. A peaceful scene, certainly, although one upheld, Caroline knew, by unremitting hard work from dawn to dusk. The cows grazing so placidly in the shade of the tall trees all had to be milked morning and evening, and the fields themselves through the passing seasons ploughed, harrowed, manured, seeded and mowed, over and over again, year after year . . . which brought her slap back to the thought of Sean, without whom she had to learn to live, through the rest of the summer, the autumn, the winter.

If it had been within her power she might have turned the bus around and gone back the way she had come, regardless of the consequences. But the big tyres hissed over the macadam and the miles slipped by, always putting more and more distance between her and the man she had so unwisely fallen in love with.

It had been, she supposed, a foolish thing to do. But how could she have helped herself? Like calls to like, and in Sean she had found the foil for her own adventurous spirit, a man unafraid of challenge on land or sea, a man, moreover, who for her posed his own challenge. How could she have resisted him? He was right for her. She needed him. It seemed a cruel irony to have found him so precipitately and unexpectedly, only to lose him because of the very deception that had brought him to her. Why could he not have accepted her, and loved her, as Caroline? Why had the shadow of Gabrielle, deceitful, immoral, beautiful Gabrielle, always come between them?

Unanswerable questions, yet her brain could not leave them alone. Plagued by them, tormented by memories of the black-haired man who had kidnapped her heart as well as her body, she sat quietly looking out of the window.

The journey ended, as journeys must. The bus pulled into the Halifax terminal and with the remainder of Sean's twenty dollars Caroline got a taxi to her apartment.

It was one of four in an older house in the south end of the city near the park. Fortunately the neighbour with whom she always left an extra key was home; ruefully explaining that she had lost all her keys, Caroline escaped as quickly as she could, for Mrs Manders, who spent too much time alone, combined a genuine kindness with an insatiable curiosity, neither of which Caroline felt able to cope with right now.

She closed the door of her apartment behind her, taking off Gabrielle's sandals and kicking them in the corner, knowing she would never wear them again. The teal-blue purse she dropped on the floor. Then she looked around her, almost as though she were a stranger entering the place for the first time.

The ceilings were high, ornamented with moulded plasterwork; when she had moved in, Caroline had redecorated in shades of antique white and ivory to heighten the sense of space and light. Throughout the apartment the floors were pale sanded hardwood. A year ago she had spent far too much money on a small Isfahan rug for the foyer; its muted blues and golds were reiterated in the abstract watercolour on the wall, gift of a friend of hers. Rug and painting were the sole furnishings in the hallway.

The living room windows faced south. Over the months she had lived there, Caroline had gradually added to her plant collection. The gracefully spreading branches of a fig tree took up one corner; on the floor and hanging from the ceiling groupings of grape ivy, palms, spider plants and vividly hued Coleus gave an impression of a garden, perfectly complementing the bamboo furniture. Her other major extravagances were a teak stereo console and a set of well-stocked teak bookshelves, the jackets of the books bright notes of colour. For her twenty-first birthday her parents had given her an exquisite silk screen print of a boat, all sweeping curves, resting on an undulating sand beach. This hung over the fireplace, gathering the warmth of sunlight into its soft yellows and golds.

Mrs Manders had done a fine job of watering the plants, Caroline thought absently, touching the soil with her fingertip, before wandering through the kitchen to her bedroom. The kitchen, unlike the rest of the apartment, was a riot of colour: brightly patterned wallpaper, red trim and accessories, ruffled red and yellow curtains. In a contrast that Caroline had decided upon purposely, the bedroom walls were a deep-toned blue, the ceiling, bedspread and trim pure white; another extravagance she allowed herself was always to have flowers in her bedroom, at present a pot of shaggy bronze chrysanthemums.

She stood in the doorway. She was home. Back where she belonged. Why then did she feel like a visitor, an alien in surroundings that should have felt familiar and welcoming?

Like an automaton, she showered and changed her clothes, shopped for a few groceries, cooked supper and cleaned up, and then wandered from room to room, picking up books and putting them down, dusting the furniture, her whole body one vast ache of loss. She was no longer self-sufficient, she thought miserably. No longer complete. She needed Sean. She wanted him to be here beside her, right now, to take her in his arms and hold her, to call her by name . . . she found she was crying, slow, hopeless tears that trickled down her cheeks and dripped on the surface of the coffee table she was polishing.

She slept fitfully that night, but she did sleep, and morning brought, if not hope, at least a new perspective. She had no idea what Sean would do when he found her gone. Would it confirm him in the belief she was indeed Gabrielle? Or would he search her out as Caroline Travers, owner of a bookstore in Halifax? She did not know. She only knew she was not ready to resume the seesaw of longing and despair that his presence seemed to mean; as Gabrielle or Caroline she was not yet prepared to see him again. Picking up the telephone by her bed, she dialled the store.

'Maryan? Caroline here. . . . Fine, thanks. Yes, I did come back a bit earlier, but I'm leaving again today. How's business?' The conversation became technical for a few minutes, then Caroline added, she hoped casually, 'By the way, someone may come looking for me, a man by the name of Sean Reilly. I don't want you to give him my address, Maryan, okay? And would you leave a memo to that effect for Elise as well? Thanks. I'll see you in a couple of weeks. 'Bye.'

Quickly she put the receiver down, knowing Maryan must be dying of curiosity. But it had had to be done. Her phone number was unlisted, so now she should be safe from discovery—assuming, of course, that Sean even bothered to look for her.

Her next phone call was to New Brunswick. A pleasant female voice said, 'Dr Frances Travers' office. May I help you?'

'Hello, Jeanie, Caroline here. Is my mother free?'

'I think she's just finishing with a patient. Hold on a minute.'

Warm and vibrant, her mother's voice came over the line. 'Caroline darling! How are you?'

Feeling absurdly as though she was seven years old again and running home with a scraped knee, Caroline gulped with something less than truth, 'Fine. Can I come and stay for a few days?'

Her mother was not one for unnecessary questions. 'Of course, we'd both love to see you. The boys are at cadet camp and Alison's still in Fredericton, so we've been feeling deserted.' Alison was Caroline's younger sister, who was working in a day-care centre for the summer. 'Today?'

'Please.'

'Lovely, darling. Go right to the house, dinner's at six-thirty. Now I've got to run, everyone and his dog seems to have decided to be ill today. 'Bye for now.'

Feeling much comforted, just as she had as a little girl, Caroline then embarked on a series of calls relating to her lost licence and credit cards, successfully hedged most of Mrs Manders' questions as she arranged to have her plants watered for another two weeks, and threw some clothes—none of them Gabrielle's—in a suitcase.

Her parents lived on the banks of the Petitcodiac River in an ultra-modern cedar and brick house that her mother adored and her father regarded with faint bemusement, as if he wasn't quite sure why he was living there. His study was his retreat when the tinted glass and angled ceilings became too much for him; it had chintz-covered armchairs, hunting prints, horse brasses, and a sheepskin rug, and smelled agreeably of tweed and tobacco. When Caroline arrived about five-thirty, parking her car in the shade of the fir trees that edged the driveway, her mother was not yet home, but her father was ensconced in the study, a mug of stout at his elbow.

A casual observer might have described Dr Frederick Travers as average: of average height and looks, he would never stand out in a crowd, and he seemed to observe the world and all in it with placid toleration. But he hid a keen brain behind his level blue eyes and, perhaps because of his apparent ordinariness, his patients had a tendency to confide in him the very problems that often lay at the root of their physical symptoms. In his own way he was just as strong-willed as his wife; slower to make up his mind, he could be immovable when he chose. Slow also to anger, his occasional explosive outbursts of temper seemed to take him as much by surprise as anyone else.

Now he said casually, as if it had been a matter of hours rather than weeks since he had seen her last, 'Hello, dear. Pour yourself a drink and come and sit down. Are you on holiday?'

'Mmm. And bored with my own company,' Caroline said lightly.

He raised a quizzical eyebrow. 'No new boy-friend in the offing?'

'I—no.' She raised her Manhattan. 'Cheers.'

'Don't know how you can drink that stuff,' her father grumbled goodnaturedly. 'Must play havoc with your digestive system. What have you been up to?'

'Oh, I spent a few days in the Digby area, went back to Halifax, and decided to come up here.' She got up restlessly and went to look out of the window, where the Petitcodiac wound through the flats, reminding her, inevitably, of a very different river. 'When are you taking your holidays this year?'

They chatted of inconsequential things until they heard the impetuous click of high heels on the parquet flooring and Caroline's mother came into the room. She threw her arms around her daughter, hugged her hard and said, 'Lovely to see you! But what have you been doing to yourself? You look——' she paused, head to one side, 'not very happy.'

Frederick would have waited until Caroline chose to confide in him; not so Fran. Impatience, as she would have been the first to admit, was her besetting sin. Her dark brown hair, in which she refused to allow any grey to show, was swept into a bun on the top of her head; her make-up, even at the end of an arduous day, was flawless and her clothes exquisite. Her second weakness, as again she would admit with an unrepentant grin, was clothes. Today she was wearing a bottle-green shirtwaist, studiedly simple in line, with jade earrings. She looked exactly what she was, a woman who loved her job, her husband, and her family.

Dropping into a chair, she gave Frederick a quick smile as he brought her a Scotch and soda. ''Lo, darling. How was your day?'

'Hellish. Yours?'

'About the same. Tell you about it later.'

Already Caroline could feel her overstretched nerves relaxing. The relationship between her dynamic mother and easygoing father had always fascinated her. Respect for each other's professional expertise often led them into long, technical medical discussions, helpful for both of them, while their personality differences occasionally caused flaming rows that seemed to cement them together rather than drive them apart. Even after nearly thirty years of marriage there was a very real physical attraction between them as well as genuine liking, and if Caroline had had to sum it up, she would have said they still had fun together.

Slipping her feet out of her pumps and tucking her ankles under her, Fran addressed Caroline. 'Tell me.'

It was half invitation, half command, little words that went back for years and covered scraped knees, lost ski races, and financial setbacks at the bookstore. 'It's a very long and peculiar story,' Caroline said slowly.

'We've half an hour until Sue serves dinner.' Sue was the live-in housekeeper who would have ruled both the Travers with a rod of iron had they allowed it.

So, haltingly at first, but then more rapidly as she lost herself in her narrative, Caroline told of the meeting with Gabrielle, the switch in clothes, and the first dinner with Sean. Of her virtual kidnapping, of Baron, and of the long slow days in the Somers' house. Of the accident to her hand, and finally of the rescue in the storm and the unexpected appearance of Joan and Ian Somers. She did not tell how she and Sean had made love; what she did say, though, was, 'The trouble is, I—I fell in love with him. Don't ask me why, he certainly gave me no encouragement, and I'm sure right up until the last day I was there he was still convinced I was Gabrielle.'

'What does he look like?' Unexpectedly, this was the first time her mother had said anything; it was unlike her to remain silent for so long.

Caroline's lips curved in a smile; almost forgetting she had an audience, she said, 'Tall, dark and handsome—it's a description that fits him perfectly. Black, black hair, grey eyes like storm clouds, a face with character, intelligence, strength. . . . Oh damn, why did I have to go and fall in love with him?'

'By the sound of him it would have been surprising if you hadn't,' Fran said wryly.

The gong sounded an imperative summons from the dining room, and obediently they all rose to their feet. Sue greeted Caroline with something approaching enthusiasm, for Caroline was her favourite of the Travers' four children, and the meal proceeded: Caesar salad, garlic shrimp in a bed of rice, fresh raspberries and cream. Not until they went back to the study did Fran ask, 'So what are you going to do? You can't stay in hiding for ever.'

'I'll go back in a few days. I just didn't want to be in Halifax right now.'

'Do you think he'll turn up at the bookstore?' This from her father.

'I don't know. It's the logical thing for him to do, I suppose.'

Fran asked curiously, 'Did he ever kiss you?'

Caroline blushed. Knowing all too well neither parent would have missed any of the implications of that, she nodded, staring down at her lap.

'He must think you're Caroline, then,' her mother said emphatically. 'He wouldn't kiss Gabrielle, not if she's done all the things you say she has.'

'I think you're wrong, Fran,' Frederick interposed. 'Gabrielle is obviously a very beautiful young woman—that has to count for something.'

Caroline suddenly found herself laughing, and knew it was just for this that she had come home. 'Thanks, Dad! You're good for the ego.'

'Anyway, once he sees you at the bookstore, he'll know you're Caroline,' Fran said triumphantly, paying no attention to either of them.

'I would have preferred him not have *needed* proof—don't you see that, Mum?' It seemed a very valid distinction to Caroline; what she had not told her parents, of course, was how Sean had called her Gabrielle only a matter of hours after making love to her.

'Well, I think you should stay here for a few days, rest up and relax—you really do look dreadful, darling, unrequited love doesn't suit you—and then go back to the store. Once you see him, maybe it will all sort itself out. You'll discover you're not in love with him after all, or he'll discover he is in love with you, or something.'

'You're an incurable romantic, Fran,' her husband remarked.

'And you love it.'

He gave her the special smile he reserved for her alone. 'Of course I do. How could I help it?'

Caroline poured herself more coffee, wondering with a catch at her heart whether she and Sean would ever have the chance to live and grow together as her parents had, to share love and laughter, hard times and good. What if he never came to the bookstore? What if she never saw him again? Her cup rattled against the saucer, for the mere thought of it was terrifying. For a mad instant she contemplated getting in her car and driving to Deep River on the chance that Sean would still be at the Somers. But what would she say if he was there? Throw herself at his feet and beg him to marry her?

Fortunately the vision this provoked resurrected a vestige of her sense of humour. The conversation changed to other matters, and in her old room under the eaves, with some of her dolls perched on the bed and the Nancy Drew and Enid Blyton books on the shelves, Caroline found herself able to sleep, buoyed up by her mother's optimism that somehow or other everything would work out.

CHAPTER TEN

As the August days passed, Caroline was not always able to regard her situation with quite as much equanimity. She missed Sean, missed him painfully. She had known him for less than three weeks, but somehow he had imprinted himself on her, so that she found herself listening for his steps, waiting to catch his deep voice, longing for his touch. Her body, unawakened before she met him, now yearned for his presence, so that sometimes at night she would lie for hour after hour remembering every detail of their lovemaking, from the smooth warmth of his skin to that last glorious assault that had ended her innocence for ever. The next day she would be heavy-eyed and tired, which did not, she was sure, escape either of her parents. But they were wise enough not to smother her with concern, merely giving her little extra attentions for which she was grateful.

The magazine her mother dropped in her lap after work one day was another of these gestures; it was a glossy fashion magazine, the model on the cover doing her best to hide her undeniable beauty beneath a bizarre hairdo and a peculiar puce shade of eye-shadow, not to mention a supercilious expression. 'It's a Canadian magazine,' Fran said briefly, sitting down on one of the lawn chairs on the patio. 'Oh, my aching feet!'

Caroline grinned at the fragile sling-back sandals her mother was discarding. 'Little wonder. Didn't your doctor ever tell you not to wear high heels all day?'

Fran smiled lazily. 'Rude brat—that's no way to talk to your mother.'

Idly Caroline flipped the pages, rather glad she wasn't committed to being fashionable if it meant

146

wearing some of these outfits, for they seemed calculated to disguise the fact that you had a figure at all. Then she stopped, her eyes riveted to the page. It was a stark black and white advertisement, the model in a rather elegant pantsuit. But it was the photographed label that held Caroline's attention, for the identical label, she knew, was on the culottes that Gabrielle had given her. Beneath the photograph she read, 'Exclusive at our boutique,' with an address on St Catherine Street in Montreal.

She felt her breathing quicken. If that particular label was indeed sold exclusively at the Montreal boutique, then Gabrielle had bought it there. Could there be any chance then that Gabrielle lived in Montreal?

'Do you really like that, darling? It's not bad, but I don't like the cut of the jacket,' Fran commented, looking over her daughter's shoulder.

Quickly Caroline explained why she had been so mesmerised by the advertisement. 'It's crazy, I suppose, but I feel like hopping on the first plane and going up there.'

'Let's!' Fran exclaimed. 'I'm off this next weekend. I could do some shopping while I was there—unless, of course, you want to go on your own?'

It was the first time Caroline had felt the slightest bit of enthusiasm for anything since she had left Deep River. 'I'd love to have your company. Will Dad want to come?'

'To shop? Goodness, no. Phone and see if we can get reservations. We could fly up Friday evening, and come back Sunday.'

And so it was that on Saturday morning at ten-thirty, Fran and Caroline were standing on the busy sidewalk of St Catherine Street, eyeing the discreet and expensive-looking façade of the Boutique Isabelle across the road. 'You can't go in,' Fran said decisively. 'They'll think you're Gabrielle. I'll go—wish me luck.'

With a faint smile on her lips Caroline watched Fran

dash across the crosswalk, wave charmingly at an irate
taxi driver just before she reached the kerb, and then
push open the leaded-glass door of the boutique and
disappear inside. Stepping back into the shade of an
awning, she composed herself to wait, knowing Fran
had never extricated herself from a good dress shop in
under half an hour. Fran was thoroughly enjoying this
expedition; she herself was less sanguine, sensing that in
a city the size of Montreal they would have to be very
lucky to turn up a trace of Gabrielle.

It was three-quarters of an hour before Fran came
out of the shop, pausing in the doorway to continue a
conversation with someone inside. She was, Caroline
noticed with amusement, loaded down with a dress box
and a bag. Then she was striding across the street, a
middle-aged woman with the vitality and élan of someone
much younger; Caroline watched her affectionately,
recognising as she had done many times before that a
lot of her own independence and zest for living was
directly attributable to Fran. 'How did you get along?'
she called.

Fran grinned. 'I'm thinking of becoming a secret
agent,' she said smugly. 'Let's go into that *pâtisserie*
and have a coffee.'

'Mum! What did you find out?'

But Fran made her daughter wait until they had sat
down and ordered. 'We'll each have a chocolate éclair,'
she said to the waitress. 'We're celebrating. Goodness,
you're impatient, Caroline!'

'I come by that honestly enough. Spill the beans,
Mother dear.'

Taking her time, Fran took a slip of paper out of
her handbag and passed it to Caroline. 'That's
Gabrielle's address,' she said with an elaborate air of
unconcern.

'Here in Montreal? How *did* you do it?'

'I lied,' said Fran, attacking the éclair with gusto. 'I
found out that Gabrielle was a fairly regular customer

there first of all. Then I said she was the daughter of a good friend of mine, and I wanted to send her a birthday gift, a sweater I'd just picked out, but I'd mislaid the address. Could they help me?' She took another bite. 'Mmm ... delicious! They couldn't have been nicer. They got me the address and I bought the sweater, so we were all happy. I made sure I'd picked out one that was my size, of course.'

'You bought more than a sweater,' accused Caroline.

'The sweetest little dress—it'll be perfect for work. Drink your tea, darling, and we'll take a cab to her apartment.'

The apartment block was at the foot of Mount Royal, a rather Gothic-looking building with square-paned windows that twinkled in the sun, and ivy creeping up the stone walls. 'That place isn't cheap,' Caroline commented. 'Drug dealing must be profitable.'

'The dress shop wasn't cheap, either. I'd better make sure I don't meet up with her, hadn't I? We wouldn't want the bird to fly the coop.' Fran asked the taxi driver to wait and then ran across the street, adjusting her dark glasses on her elegant little nose.

The wait was only five minutes this time, and as Fran approached the taxi, she gave Caroline the victory sign. Quickly telling the driver the address of their hotel, she sat back in the seat, shoving her glasses up on her hair. 'It was the right place. I spoke to the concierge and he told me Gabrielle was away and wouldn't be back until next week.'

Caroline eyed her mother suspiciously. 'You'd better tell me how much that cost.'

'Ten dollars. For which he agreed to forget that I'd been there.'

Caroline fished in her wallet and gave Fran a ten-dollar bill, her brain working overtime. So Gabrielle was run to ground. Somehow, before next week, she had to get that piece of news to Sean. 'Would you mind very much if we changed our reservations? If we went home this evening, then I could drive back to Halifax tomorrow.'

'I wouldn't mind a bit. There's a marvellous lingerie shop next door to the hotel. I'll go there while you're phoning the ticket office.'

There were seats available on the evening flight, they were home by ten, and Caroline slept like a log the whole night through. By noon the next day she was packed and ready to leave, her parents accompanying her out to the car. She hugged them both affectionately. 'Thanks for putting up with me, I don't think I was very good company.'

'You don't have to be,' Frederick said comfortably, tamping the tobacco in his pipe. 'That's what home's for.'

She knew he meant exactly what he had said. ''Bye, Dad, Mum. Take care, and thanks for all your help.'

'It was fun,' Fran said cheerfully. 'Good luck, darling. Bring him home to meet us, won't you?'

Fran's blithe assumption that this would be possible made Caroline's throat tighten. 'I hope so,' she said fervently. One last hug and she got in the car, reversing down the driveway and waving as she turned on to the road.

As the car steadily covered the miles between Moncton and Halifax, she found herself humming in tune to the radio. Bless her parents, she thought with heartfelt gratitude. They were so dependable, always there when she needed them, yet otherwise not attempting to run her life. And it had been that way as long as she could remember, a combination of support and detachment that had been a major factor in her rise to success in the highly competitive world of skiing. She was very fortunate. . . .

But there was more to her good mood than that. If— no, she thought determinedly—when Sean came to the bookstore, she would have concrete information for him, an address where in a few days' time he could track down the real Gabrielle. And maybe, just maybe, he'd be able to free Martin. Refusing to dwell on the alternative that Sean might have dropped out of her life as suddenly as he had entered it, she kept driving, anxious to get back to the apartment.

This time it welcomed her back. Her spider plants were sending out shoots with great abandon, while the Tradescantia was covered with tiny mauve blooms. She watered and sprayed them, picking off any dead leaves, to the accompaniment of the last act of *Aida*, letting herself enjoy all the memories of Sean. His laugh when she had said something to amuse him; the pain in his face when he had talked about Martin; the almost agonised intensity of feeling in the grey eyes as his body had found its release in hers. So many memories. *Let there be more*, she prayed silently.

Enjoying the peace and solitude of the apartment, she cooked a light supper, afterwards reading in the living room, Rachmaninoff's Second Piano Concerto all the company she wanted if she could not have Sean's. *Tomorrow, maybe* ... this was the thought that she took to bed.

Originally Caroline had not planned to be back at work until Wednesday of that week, so when she went in first thing on Monday morning she was a full two days early; because of the importance of seeing Sean, it would have taken far more than the usual herd of wild horses to keep her away. She parked her car in the lot outside the mall and walked across the tarmac, the morning breeze teasing her hair. She had dressed with considerable care in a sky-blue linen blouse and coffee-coloured skirt of the same fabric, a wide brown leather belt around her waist. Her shoes were thin-strapped sandals of the identical shade as the belt; had she but known it, she looked very much Fran's daughter.

Maryan was already in the store, although it was half an hour until opening time. Hearing the key turn in the lock, she looked up in surprise. She was a girl who to her sorrow was usually called cute rather than beautiful; she had a mop of black curls, an upturned nose, and a delightfully infectious laugh which she now produced, 'Hi, Caroline. You're back early—don't tell me you missed the place!'

Caroline smiled and temporised, 'I may take a couple of days off later in the month. How are you? Have you been busy?'

'Very busy. Sales are well up over last month already.' They went into the little office at the back of the store, and within a relatively short time Caroline felt up-to-date again. 'You've done well,' she said warmly. 'How's Elise working out?' Elise had been hired only five weeks ago as temporary summer help.

'Pretty well,' Maryan said judiciously. 'A slight tendency to gravitate towards the male customers. Nothing really serious, although you should have seen her when your friend arrived—she nearly flipped. Mind you, I did, too—what a hunk!'

'My friend?' Caroline pressed her fingertips hard against the desk top.

'Yes, the one you warned me about—Sean Reilly. He's been here twice.' Maryan eyed Caroline sideways. 'If he'd been looking for me, I'd have given him my address. Or anything else he asked for, for that matter.'

'Would you now?' Caroline responded, trying to steady her erratic heartbeat. 'When was he here?'

'The day after you phoned. Then again last week, on the offchance, he said, that you'd come back early. I told him then you wouldn't be around until this Wednesday. If I'd known you'd be here today, I'd have told him. Sorry.'

'It's all right.' Her throat was dry. Trying hard to sound offhand, Caroline asked, 'Did he say he'd come back again?'

Maryan frowned. 'Well, not in so many words. But

'm sure he will. If he was interested enough to come wice, I don't imagine he'd stop there.'

'Well, we'll have to see, won't we?' said Caroline with an assumption of briskness. She looked at her watch. Time to open. I'll unlock the door.'

It wasn't difficult for her to be busy all day, for there was a lot of paperwork to catch up on and more than the usual number of customers, the mall being crowded with summer tourists. Twice she thought she heard Sean's deep voice and each time her heart thumped in her breast: a most uncomfortable sensation, despite whatever the romantic poets might say about it. Neither man was Sean; the first was an overweight professor wanting a book on medieval architecture, the second a bearded young man interested in a self-sufficient existence on two acres or less. At six-thirty Caroline went back to the apartment, which did not seem quite as welcoming as it had the evening before. Nor did Sean come on Tuesday.

On Wednesday Caroline put on the same outfit she had worn on Monday; after all, Maryan had told Sean she'd be returning to work today. The morning dragged by, scarcely enough customers to justify one of them being there, let alone two. But at eleven-thirty it seemed as though everyone in Halifax had suddenly decided to buy a book. Maryan took over the cash register, while Caroline scurried around answering questions, digging out books that hadn't been requested for months, and taking down a variety of esoteric orders. Then a new customer, a rather ferocious-looking gentleman with a military haircut whom she immediately labelled as an ex-army officer asked for a copy of Pierre Berton's latest paperback, and when she checked Caroline found the last copy on the shelves had been sold. 'Just a moment, please,' she said. 'I know I have some out back.'

She hurried to the stockroom. Naturally the books were on the very top shelf, they always were on a busy day. She pulled over the steps, hauled a fair number of the books out of the box, and clambered down. Balancing them carefully, she went back into the store, wishing she hadn't worn high-heeled sandals no matter if they did match her belt—her feet were killing her. And then she saw him. He was standing in the middle of the store, looking right at her. Unsmiling, grey eyes guarded.

She tripped over the edge of the carpet, the books went flying, and she said, loudly enough that a ripple of laughter went over the shop, 'Oh, *damn*!'

She bent to pick them up, her cheeks scarlet; if she had visualised this meeting between her and Sean, she had pictured herself very cool, very collected, very much in control.

Kneeling beside her, Sean said *sotto voce*, 'Do you always throw the books at the customers?'

Very much aware that the military gentleman who had requested the book was standing nearby and was no doubt listening to every word, she muttered, 'If I do, you're a prime candidate.'

'Oh, I'm not a customer.' He gave her the last of the books. 'I'm here for quite another reason.'

'Then you'll have to wait.' She smiled brightly at the General: he must have been at least a General, with those frosty blue eyes. 'Here you are, sir. Sorry about the delay.'

'Humph.' The white moustache quivered. 'Rather a lot of money for a paperback, isn't it?'

'I'm afraid the prices of books are no exception to the general inflationary trend,' Caroline answered as diplomatically as she could.

'Would have paid that much for a hardcover a few years ago. Disgraceful!' He handed the book back to her. 'Have to think about it.' A sharp nod and he left the store.

Left with the armload of books and her mouth open, Caroline did not dare look at Sean, for if she had, she would have begun to laugh hysterically. Grimly she headed for the B's, to shelve the rejected paperbacks.

'Can we have lunch together?'

Sounding harassed rather than collected, she replied, 'If we're this busy, I may not be able to get away.'

'They're thinning out already.'

'I've only got an hour.'

'That'll be long enough.'

Did he mean he didn't want to be with her for longer than an hour? Or did he mean anything he had to say could be said in less than an hour? A meaningless smile fixed on her lips, Caroline went to the rescue of a flustered young mother whose small son seemed intent on eating the wares on the lowest shelf, and then said to Maryan, 'Can you manage for an hour? I think the worst is over.'

'Don't rush back,' said Maryan with embarrassing promptness; she had, Caroline knew, taken in every detail of the meeting with the black-haired man who three times had come to the store to find Caroline.

'I'll be back by one,' Caroline said firmly, taking her handbag from under the counter and preceding Sean out of the bookshop.

He took her by the elbow in a no-nonsense grip that nevertheless seemed to sear through her blouse. Perhaps she should have pulled away. It would have been the sensible thing to do. But she did not want to. To be touched by him again, even in so practical and unromantic a way, was at the moment all she asked.

The restaurant was on the second floor of the mall, and it was crowded. By dint of smiling at the waitress, Sean procured a corner table for them, although it was cramped enough that Caroline had a potted palm drooping over one shoulder, while the large blonde lady eating alone at the next table was much too close for comfort. She was already eyeing them with interest; presumably they looked more promising than the dispirited meat pie on her plate.

Unable to think of anything to say, Caroline ran her eyes rapidly over the menu. 'Club sandwich and coffee—they can't really ruin those even if they try.'

Sean did not even bother looking. 'I'll have the same.'

He rested his forearms on the not-very-clean tablecloth, and with a quick upward glance under her lashes, Caroline saw he was wearing a light blue V-necked sweater over a white shirt, the collar open. Quickly she lowered her eyes, remembering how her head had rested in the hollow of his throat, how warm his skin had been. . . . She said at random, 'Are you feeling better?'

'Yes. I was lucky, all I got was a hell of a cold.'

There was still a trace of huskiness in his voice. 'How's Baron?'

'Fine——' The waitress arrived, he gave their order, and then he said urgently, 'Caroline, I——'

She could not help herself. 'I'm not Gabrielle any more?'

'No, you're not Gabrielle,' he answered very quietly. 'You never were, were you? It was only I who was convinced you were.' He looked straight at her. 'The first thing I owe you is an apology.'

'For making love to me?' And she could have bitten off her tongue.

The blonde lady had given up any pretence of eating. Sean gave her an exasperated look and then answered in French, 'I'm not sure I shall ever apolgise for that—it may have been the only thing I did right the whole time you were there.'

Caroline was playing with her fork, digging it into the tablecloth in a manner not calculated to improve it. Also speaking French, she replied, 'I don't see how you can say that. In effect, you made love to a woman you loathe.'

Over the table his hand reached for hers; she jerked it back and the fork went flying, causing a disproportionate clatter on the floor. Their blonde neighbour made a great to-do about bending over to reach it and then passing it to Sean, who accepted it with more grace than Caroline could have mustered. Then he grinned across the table at his companion. 'This is pretty hopeless, isn't it?' His smile faded. 'I feel very strange sitting here across from you. It's as though I know you and yet you're a stranger, not who I thought you were. A mixture of the known and the unknown. Caroline. Caroline Travers, who owns a bookstore and loves a challenge. Who's brave and impatient and touchingly beautiful.'

The waitress plunked the two plates in front of them and sloshed coffee in their cups. The little containers of cream, Caroline noticed resignedly, had in neat letters across the top, Edible Petroleum Product.

'Are you even listening to me?' Sean demanded.

'Yes, I'm listening. 'I—I just don't know what to say, that's all.'

'I'm sorry I thought you were Gabrielle. I frightened you, set the dog on you, kept you confined . . . all I can say is that I'm sorry. If it's any use, I hated every minute of it. Even when I was convinced you were Gabrielle, I hated it. But I had to do it, because of Martin.'

In a small voice, Caroline said, 'I know where Gabrielle is.'

He leaned forward. '*What* did you say?'

'I know where Gabrielle is. Or at least where she should be by now.'

'*Where?*'

'In Montreal, in an apartment building near Mount Royal.' She gave him the exact address. 'She was away, but the concierge said she'd be back this week.'

Sean looked dazed with shock. 'How the devil did you find that out?'

Briefly Caroline described the advertisement in the magazine, and told how she and her mother had gone to the boutique and then to the apartment building. 'Mother tipped the concierge so he wouldn't tell Gabrielle anyone was asking for her,' she finished, fiddling with her sandwich so she wouldn't have to look at him.

'I'll get the first flight up there,' said Sean, an edge of excitement in his voice. 'I'll have her followed, and with a bit of luck we'll catch her red-handed. Caroline, I had no idea that you'd have news like this. I figured I'd lost track of her for good.'

'If you catch her with drugs on her, will that mean you can get Martin out of prison?'

'It'll reopen the whole case.' He rubbed at his forehead, giving his head a little shake. 'I still can't believe it.'

The sandwich tasted like sawdust. Caroline chewed and swallowed automatically, saying with careful casualness, 'I hope it will mean Martin gets freed.'

'Yes. So do I. . . . This is lousy coffee, isn't it?'

She was not deceived by his attempted offhandedness, for she of all people knew how deeply he longed for his brother's freedom. 'We should have something stronger to drink to your success.'

'I'll succeed, Caroline, if it's the last thing I do,' he answered, his mouth grim with purpose.

She felt alarm quiver along her nerves. 'Be careful, won't you?'

'Don't you worry about me, I'm used to looking after myself.'

She wanted to cry, *I can't help worrying about you*. In case she was tempted, she took a big mouthful of the sandwich.

'Caroline, look at me.'

Unwillingly she did as she was asked, her dark blue eyes wary. To give herself something to do, she picked up her coffee mug, curling both hands around it.

His grey eyes very direct, he said, 'You do understand that I have to go straight to Montreal and find Gabrielle? Because of Martin, that takes precedence. I don't know how long I'll be. It may only take a day or two, it may take weeks. However long it takes, I'll have to see it through.'

He paused, as if he wanted a response from her. 'Precedence over what?' she asked.

'Over my seeing more of you, of course.'

He had forgotten to speak in French; their neighbour, Caroline noticed, was now eating her dessert with elaborate slowness. It was a gooey edifice of yellow sponge cake, soggy-looking strawberries, and heaped-up artifical cream, which, judging by the woman's girth, she should not have been eating at all. With a singular lack of feeling in her voice Caroline said, 'Oh. I see.' Which was a lie.

'Are you pleased to see me again?'

Her lashes flickered upwards and then quickly hid her eyes again. 'I—yes, of course.' She was trying so hard to keep the blaze of emotion from her words that she only sounded colourless—and totally unconvincing.

Sean said impatiently, 'Look, I know our relationship got off to a bad start——'.

A little devil in her tongue drove her to say, 'I wasn't aware we had a relationship, Sean.'

'I slept with you, didn't I?'

This time it was the blonde woman who dropped her fork. Caroline gave a nervous start, but Sean was not to be deflected. 'Didn't I?' he repeated.

To hell with their neighbour. What Sean was saying was far more important than an eavesdropping blonde. 'With me or with Gabrielle?' she asked bodly.

'Back to square one. Caroline, I swear——'

'Do you want to see the dessert menu, sir?'

Grimacing in annoyance, he waved the waitress away. 'No, thanks. Just bring us the bill.'

Caroline began fishing in her purse. 'I'll pay for mine.'

'Don't be so bloody independent!'

'I *am* independent.'

'The least I can do is buy you lunch.'

She looked down at her half-eaten sandwich and the unfinished coffee, which tasted far worse lukewarm than it had hot, and a smile tugged at the corners of her mouth, the first genuine smile she had given him since he had walked into the bookstore. 'You should be able to do better than this. Taking everything into consideration.'

He was quick to catch her change of mood. 'You think a mere kidnapping deserves better than a club sandwich? You have expensive tastes, Caroline Travers.'

The laughter in his eyes drove everything else out of her mind. She said recklessly, 'I think it deserves a dinner for two when you get back.'

'Somewhere other than here.'

'Indeed.' She might as well be hanged for a sheep as a lamb. 'An intimate dinner. By candlelight.'

'You're on,' he grinned. 'I might even wear a suit. Do you realise I've never seen you in a dress?'

'I have one. I'll dust it off and wear it,' she replied pertly.

Now when he reached for her hand, she let hers lie still under his, willing her fingers not to tremble. Sean said seriously, 'I promise we'll have that dinner, Caroline, and I hope it will be soon.'

'So do I,' she gulped, hoping he couldn't feel the racing of her pulse.

'Thank God . . . I was beginning to be afraid I'd done the wrong thing in coming back to see you again.'

'No. No, you didn't do that.' But her lashes were still hiding her eyes.

He looked at his watch and said ruefully, 'Your hour's nearly up, and I've got to get to a phone and book a reservation. Or I might even drive up—that way I'd have a car and I could take Baron. We'd better go.'

She followed him through the closely spaced tables to he cash register, very much aware that the blonde was unabashedly staring after them. After Sean paid the bill, they went out into the mall, which was thronged with casually dressed shoppers and salespeople on their lunch breaks: not the ambience for a conversation of any intimacy or significance, Caroline realised with something akin to despair. In a few moments Sean would be leaving her again, and it might be weeks before she saw him again. . . .

By a kind of mutual consent they stopped outside the bookstore, edging over to the wall to get out of the way of the crowds. A small boy was throwing a very noisy tantrum only a few yards away, his distracted mother repeating ineffectively, 'Now, Dougie, be good—I'll tell your father on you if you don't. Be a good boy, Dougie, and stop screaming this minute!'

Sean had been staring at this little scene with a kind of horrified fascination. 'If I ever have a son, he won't get away with that kind of behaviour,' he said decisively.

Her imagination, which was always rather apt to run away with her, instantly presented her with a picture of a black-haired child with a chin as stubborn as Sean's and eyes—eyes of a dark, dark blue. She felt the heat creep into her cheeks and looked up to find Sean regarding her with as much interest as, a moment ago, he had been watching the little boy. He said gravely, 'I don't know enough about heredity to know if he'd have black hair or auburn, do you?'

Her jaw dropped. 'N—no, I—I guess I don't.'

'Look it up while I'm gone.' He sobered, dropping his hands on her shoulders. 'Caroline, I'll be back as soon as I can. I'll drop you a note once I have some idea of how long it'll be. We'll continue this conversation then, that's a promise. Take care of yourself, won't you?'

'Yes,' she whispered, although the eyes she raised to

him were full of uncertainty. 'You do the same. Goo
luck.'

'Thanks.' Oblivious to the jostling crowds, he said fo
her ears alone, 'Do you remember I once said you ha
the voice of an angel and a beauty that drove me crazy
That hasn't changed.' Giving her no chance to answe
he very deliberately bent his head and kissed he
thoroughly and at considerable length.

Two teenagers emitted ear-splitting wolf whistles.
little girl said to her mother in a piercing treble, 'Why
he kissing her, Mum?' But Sean did not release Carolin
until he was ready. 'He's kissing her because he likes it
he murmured, his teasing words belied by the primitiv
passion blazing in his eyes.

For Caroline it had been a kiss of mingled pain an
pleasure. She had no need to wonder at the pleasure
loving Sean as she did. The pain, she knew, stemmed fron
the question he had asked her. She remembered all to
well him telling her she had the voice of an angel; he ha
hated himself for saying it, for he had thought he wa
speaking to Gabrielle. Did *he* not remember that? Or di
he not think it was a distinction of any importance? Wer
she and Gabrielle so confused in his mind that he coul
not separate one from the other? Which led to the fina
inevitable question, the one she had already asked him
and that he had not answered. With which one of then
had he thought he was making love?

As these thoughts were racing through her brain, ou
of the corner of her eye she caught sight of Maryar
gazing at them both, spellbound, from her stance by th
cash register, and of one of her regular customer
observing them with equal interest. Gratefully sh
seized on this for something to say. 'You're ruining m
reputation,' she sputtered.

'Good,' Sean said unrepentently. 'Caroline, I——' H
halted in frustration. 'Hell, there's too much to say an
no time to say it. But I swear we'll have the time when
get back. We'll begin all over again. . . .'

Between them the air was over-loud with things unsaid, things that were not going to be said, not now. Because she did not know how else to handle the situation, Caroline said with attempted lightness, 'We'll get the maître d' to introduce us. Mr Sean Reilly, this is Miss Caroline Travers. Miss Travers, Mr Reilly.'

'That's a fine idea.' He gave her a quick hug. 'I'll be in touch. Don't go on any rooftops while I'm gone.'

Before she could think of any reply to this, he had turned on his heel and was threading his way purposely through the crowds towards the nearest door. It opened and closed, and he was lost from sight; he had not looked back. Her emotions in a turmoil, Caroline stared after him. Joy because she had seen him again, frustration because it had been so brief and inconclusive a meeting, pain because he was no longer with her and her arms were empty again. *I love him. But does he love me?*

He had been pleased to see her. He wanted to see her again. But that might have nothing to do with love. After all, maybe he just wanted to sleep with her again. The thought sent a jolt of agony through her whole body.

'Afternoon, Miss Travers. Have you—er—lost something?'

She dragged her eyes away from the door to the face of the elderly gentleman who was addressing her. He was one of her favourite customers, a retired coastguard captain who was a voracious reader; often she had delivered books to the tiny house in the south end where he lived with his frail, white-haired wife and an astonishingly foul-mouthed parrot. 'Hello, Captain Simms.' She said the first words that came into her head. 'I—how long have you and your wife been married?'

He was only momentarily taken aback. Faded blue eyes twinkling, he said, 'Fifty-four years come September.'

'And did you know right away that you wanted t
marry her?'

'The minute I laid eyes on her.'

It hadn't been quite that quick with her ... bu
almost. And what of Sean, who the first time he ha
seen her had thought she was Gabrielle?

Captain Simms cleared his throat. 'Couldn't hel
noticing the man you were—ahem, talking to. H
looked like a good match for you. Touch of th
adventurer there, I wouldn't be surprised.'

'More than a touch.'

'That's what you need, my girl. Don't you marr
some nice young fellow who works in an office an
likes to spend his evenings watching televisior
Wouldn't do for you at all.' He added gruffly, 'The wif
and I saw you in a restaurant three or four months ag
with a tall, fair-haired man. Didn't look the right typ
for you. Worried me a bit.'

That would have been Richard. 'He's past history,
Caroline said firmly.

'Hope this other one isn't.'

'I hope not, too,' she answered fervently. Tucking he
arm in the Captain's, she walked into the store with
him, knowing Maryan wouldn't dare ask any question
while she was with a customer. 'Sorry I'm late!' sh
called. 'Go for lunch now, and take your time.'

Captain Simms wanted a book on furniture refinish
ing, the phone started to ring, and two people wer
waiting at the cash register. Thrusting Sean to the bacl
of her mind, Caroline got to work.

CHAPTER ELEVEN

IT was a good thing Caroline had the business to occupy her over the next few days. For a week she heard nothing from Sean. She missed him so acutely that she was frightened by the depth of her own emotion, and by her vulnerability; it was a facet of love she had never understood before, and certainly never experienced. She did not know where he was, nor did she know what he was doing. She had no real fear that he would involve himself in any kind of romantic liaison with Gabrielle; unless, that was Gabrielle had the same effect on him as she, Caroline, did, a thought she shied away from. What she really worried about was Gabrielle's connection with the drug scene, and the danger this might cause to Sean who was so bent on bringing her to justice. Caroline had read enough newspapers and magazines to know that drug-dealing was a business where millions of dollars were at stake and lives were held cheap. That one of these might be Sean's was another thought she could not bear to contemplate.

Over and over again she went over all the details of their luncheon together, trying to wrest every nuance from each word that had been said, realising more and more clearly how much had not been said. Hinted at, maybe, referred to obliquely, but not said outright. He had talked of a red-haired son . . . but had he really meant he wanted Caroline to be the mother of his child? While the prospect made her tremble with a happiness beyond any imagining, and while at times she was convinced that was exactly what he had meant, there were other times when she was not so sure. He had never told her he loved her, and surely that should come first?

Because her mind was rarely completely on what she was doing—something else she secretly deplored, for up until now her powers of concentration had never failed her—she sent a batch of orders to the wrong publishing houses, mislaid some very important receipts, and four times in as many days gave customers entirely the wrong books. Maryan, who was plainly bursting with curiosity but had so far managed to exhibit a commendable degree of restraint, re-ordered the books and found the bundle of receipts on the top shelf of the closet where the cleaning supplies were kept. 'But I couldn't have put them there!' Caroline wailed.

'Perhaps Mrs Courtney picked them up and thought that would be a good place for them,' Maryan said soothingly. Mrs Courtney was their cleaning lady.

'Mrs Courtney never picks up anything she doesn't have to, you know that as well as I do.' Caroline mimicked Mrs Courtney's nasal whine. 'Oh, I couldn't do that. Against the union rules, dearie . . . it must have been me, Maryan. Honestly, I'm losing my grip.'

'Must be love,' Maryan said fliply.

Caroline blushed, muttered something cross and incomprehensible under her breath, and went to clean up her desk. The day dragged on.

But on the Thursday, eight days after Sean had left, a letter from Montreal arrived for Caroline care of the bookstore. Maryan always sorted the mail. Without comment she handed Caroline the envelope with the address in an angular, obviously masculine handwriting, and Personal scrawled across one corner.

Caroline took it, her hand not quite steady, and shoved it in her pocket, and as luck would have it was so inundated with customers that it was over an hour before she was able to retreat to the back room, close the door, and tear open the envelope. The notepaper was cream-coloured and expensive, the ink very black; it did not take long to discern Sean had been in a hurry when he had written to her.

Caroline,
Three of us keeping a watch on Gabrielle day and night. So far nothing. Sooner or later she's got to make a contact, but I'll have to stay here until she does. Think about you. Miss you.

                                        Sean.

Caroline sat down rather abruptly in the office chair, which, as always, squeaked beneath her weight so that she thought automatically, *I must remember to grease it.*

More slowly she read the letter again, not that it took long. He was thinking about her and he missed her. But there was no *Dear* Caroline. No *Love*, Sean. No mention of when he might return to Halifax, and certainly no address or phone number at the top of the letter. Knowing his hands had touched the paper, she held it to her cheek, but she felt nothing. She didn't want a hurried, uncommunicative letter, she thought dully. She wanted Sean himself, his devil-may-care smile and his silky black hair, his warm hands and lean, hard body. What good was a letter in comparison to that?

Another week passed. The weekend dragged by, Sunday the worst day because she could not go to the store and hence there was no chance she would see him. Monday was normally her day off, but she went in anyway. On Tuesday she slept in, because she had forgotten to set her alarm; when she did wake it was pouring rain, which suited her mood, she thought sourly as she dragged herself out of bed. Determined to feel sorry for herself, she put on an unflattering black dress that she had mistakenly bought at a sale, and no jewellery, nor did she bother with make-up because she was so late.

Tuesday was Maryan's day off, so at least Caroline had plenty to do all day, and by five-thirty, which was closing time, she was tired out. The store was empty, so she went into the office for her keys to lock up, slipping her feet out of her high-heeled shoes with a sigh of relief as she stood in the doorway.

'Want to go for dinner? An intimate dinner for two?'

Two things happened simultaneously: the keys flew from her hand and disappeared under a set of shelves, and the colour drained from her face. 'You—scared, me, Sean,' she whispered, with only partial truth. 'I thought the store was empty.'

He was wearing a beige trench coat that was damp from the rain, and dark trousers with a black crew-neck sweater. Although there was only a faint smile on his mouth, his eyes were blazingly alive with an emotion whose source she could not guess. He looked very fit, very tough, and very masculine, and she had never been happier to see anyone in her life before. Her instinctive urge was to run and fling her arms around him; she fought it down, deeply uncertain of what to expect from him.

'You look pale,' he remarked, making no attempt to close the distance between them as he ran his eyes up and down her figure in the severe black dress. 'Are you contemplating entering a nunnery?'

Thankfully she followed his lead. 'Perhaps I should,' she answered demurely, lowering her lashes and gazing with becoming modesty at her stockinged feet. 'Do you think I show signs of a vocation?'

'I think you should delay your decision for twenty-four hours.' A gleam of his white teeth. 'A lot can happen in twenty-four hours.'

She was blushing again, damn it, she thought with rather unnunlike profanity. 'When did you get back?' she said banally.

He consulted his watch. 'Three minutes forty-five seconds ago. Are you finished here?'

'I was finished at nine o'clock this morning . . . just let me lock up and count the cash, and I'll be ready to leave.'

Caroline totalled the cash three times, got three

different answers, and at random picked one of them to write in the account book. Putting on her shoes, she got her coat and umbrella, and then held out a twenty-dollar bill to Sean. 'I owe you this.'

He grinned at her. 'Returning stolen goods, huh? I'm not sure the nuns will approve of that kind of behaviour.' He let his eyes drop to her mouth, then linger on the slim line of her throat. 'Not to mention any of the other behaviour you've indulged in when with me!'

Her heart caught in her throat. She would *not* blush again. She would not. She said primly, 'Such as climbing on rooftops.'

'I wasn't really referring to that.'

She glared at him, holding out the bill. 'I know you weren't. Take the wretched money and be quiet!'

He shoved it in his pocket. 'By the way, it was thoughtful of you to park the car in front of the police station that day—I don't think I ever thanked you, did I?'

'I knew you'd appreciate it.'

In exactly the same tone of voice, he said, 'We belong together, you and I, Caroline—you do realise that, don't you?'

Her mouth dropped open. She shut it, swallowed hard, and spoke the literal truth. 'Yes. Although you're worse than I am.' A strange thing to say to the man she was in love with, but she was sure he would know what she meant.

'Nonsense. Who sat on the roof waving a towel over her head?'

'Who kidnapped me in the first place?'

'Best mistake I ever made. Which reminds me, I've got a lot to tell you. Let's get out of here.'

He still had not touched her. Nevertheless, now that she was over the first shock, Caroline's heart was singing from the sheer joy of seeing him again. And, as he had said, a lot can happen in twenty-four hours. What it would be, she had no idea. Oddly enough, she was not even in a great hurry to find out. *What will be will be* ... and as long as she was with Sean, that was enough. Her eyes velvet-soft, her lips smiling, she followed him out of the bookstore and carefully locked the door.

'The car's this way. Baron will be pleased to see you.'

They ran across the wet tarmac to the red Porsche. Baron was squeezed in behind the seats along with Sean's suitcase, and thumped his thick tail against the leather as they got in the car, his big white-fanged jaws laughing. And then Sean touched her, but only to lay his hand on her sleeve and say loudly, 'Friend, Baron. Friend.' To Caroline he added, 'Don't want him still thinking he's got to keep you under lock and key.'

He turned on the ignition and the wipers swished across the windows. But before leaving, Sean half turned towards Caroline, his eyes devouring her face as if he would re-learn every contour of it, although all he said was, 'Do you like walking in the rain?'

'Love it!'

'Good. Yet another reason why we belong together. I don't know Halifax that well—where can we go?'

'Point Pleasant Park. Turn right at the lights and then left at the next intersection.'

As he drove towards the exit, he remarked, 'I ended up taking the car to Montreal, so today Baron and I have been cooped up all day. Both of us need to stretch our legs.'

She gave him directions as they went along, and within fifteen minutes they were parked by the container pier. They got out, Baron scrambling to the ground, tail wagging. It was more of a thick drizzle than rain by now, the waters of the harbour clothed in fog, and the air heavy with the mingled scent of the ocean and the wet pine trees. Sean pulled a big black umbrella from the back of the car, put it up, and tucked Caroline's arm in his so that they were both sheltered from the rain. While the dog stood patiently waiting, he smiled down at her. 'Hello, Caroline.'

There was nothing in the world but a pair of steady grey eyes. She said breathlessly, 'Hello yourself. Welcome back.'

'It's good to be back.'

It was hardly a scintillating conversation, but the simple words were, for now, all Caroline wanted to hear. Knowing from the expression on his face that he was going to kiss her, she tilted her face upwards and closed her eyes as his mouth found hers. Because he was holding the umbrella, he had not put his arms around her; it was only their lips that touched and clung.

For Caroline time stopped. A moment ago she had said welcome back. What she should have said was welcome home, because to have him here with her made her world complete.

As Sean slowly moved back, Baron gave an exaggeratedly loud yawn at their feet. It was impossible not to laugh, and the tenderness of their kiss slipped into the past, although, Caroline thought with sudden confidence, it must surely be a portent of the future.

When they had walked down on to the beach, where little waves lapped at the rocks and the mournful dirge of the foghorn boomed through the mist, she asked, 'How did you get along?'

'We got her,' and he did not need to say whom he meant. 'It took long enough, but in the end we did. I'd hired two private detectives, because I knew I couldn't watch her all the time, and they'd been following a couple of guys we were sure were her contacts. The police were really interested in one of them but had never been able to pin anything on him. So one night both contacts went to her apartment together—a bad mistake on their part. The police went to the apartment with a search warrant and found drugs on the two men and a small fortune in cocaine and L.S.D. stashed away in Gabrielle's bedroom. So we got all three of them for possession and trafficking. She won't get out of that in a hurry, I'll tell you.'

'And what about Martin? How will that help him?'

'I went to see him on the way back to tell him what had happened. I thought he'd still argue with me and try and convince me that Gabrielle was a poor, wronged innocent. But he didn't. Maybe he'd had enough time to think now, and to realise someone had to plant that dope in his kitbag and the obvious person was Gabrielle. Anyway, he's going to make a full statement to the police and his case will be re-opened. I spoke to a topnotch lawyer in Montreal who's had experience in these cases, and he said Martin will be fully pardoned and freed.'

As tears crowded Caroline's eyes, she blinked them back. She had never met Martin, but somehow, through Sean, felt as though she had, and the news of his release seemed to lift a weight from her mind. More often than had been comfortable she had had this vision of a bearded young man pacing back and forth in his cell, trying to keep the walls at bay; he would not have to do it for much longer. 'You must be happy about that,' she said inadequately.

'Yes.' They were further along the peninsula now, where the breakers were rolling in from the harbour to collapse in a tumble of foam on the rocky shore. A gull swooped out of the mist and Baron raced after it, a hopeless chase if ever there was one. Sean chuckled. 'He never learns that wings are faster than legs.'

'He looks beautiful when he's running.'

Sean began telling her how he had managed to acquire Baron from the police three years ago, which led Caroline to describe the Irish wolfhound her father had once owned. From there the talk moved to their respective families. They had circled along another path and were heading back to the car when Sean said abruptly, 'You know, I've hated Gabrielle ever since I found out what happened to Martin. I didn't like her the first time I met her, she didn't ring true, and as soon as I found out about the border crossing, I knew she was at the bottom of it. But when I saw her being arrested in the apartment, I almost felt sorry for her. Because she'd been greedy for material things, and unscrupulous and un-imaginative enough to get involved in drug dealing as a way of getting them, she's ruined her life. She looked pinched and old when they took her away . . . I won't forget that picture of her for a while.'

'Perhaps it's as well you don't hate her any more,' Caroline said slowly. 'Hate can be a very destructive emotion.'

'That's true . . . did I ever tell you that besides being beautiful and brave, you're also very wise?' She smiled shyly, the glow of pleasure in her eyes all the answer he needed. 'Let me tell you something else,' he went on. 'The minute I saw her I wondered how I could ever have mistaken you for her. Oh, there are superficial likenesses, for sure—in your facial structure and your hair colour and so on. But your eyes are far more beautiful, and your hair is curly.' He grinned at her, for it was indeed curling in little tendrils around her face from all the dampness in the air.

'It's a real nuisance sometimes. I've often wished I had sleek, smooth, manageable hair like Gabrielle's.'

He tweaked a curl over her ear, his face preoccupied. 'But there's more to the difference than that, Caroline. I think it's a difference of expression. Her way of life shows in her face. She looks hard as nails underneath all that make-up, as if she'd turn in her own grandmother if it would make her a buck. Her mouth is thin, and she doesn't smile like you with her whole heart. Her smiles are calculated, just enough to get her what she wants. I don't know how I could have been such a fool as to have taken you for her.'

'Well, I did start out by doing my best to convince you I was her,' Caroline said fairly.

'You couldn't convince me of that now in a million years. I'll never look at you again and see her.'

There was such passionate conviction in his voice that Caroline knew he meant every word of it. 'I'm glad,' she said simply. 'I wouldn't want to think that I'd be a constant reminder of her.' Then she stopped in confusion, wondering if she had implied that she and Sean would be seeing a lot of each other in the future; heaven knows, she wanted to, but she couldn't very well tell *him* that.

'You never will be again.'

But she had been in the past. When they had made love, for instance.... Not watching where she was going, she stepped in a puddle and said crossly, 'Darn it!'

'Your shoes are soaked. We'd better get back to the car.' Sean whistled for the dog.

They took a short cut through the trees, Caroline's feet slithering on the wet pine needles, little showers of water dripping from the sodden boughs overhead. Back at the car park Sean unlocked her door and let Baron in on his side. Getting in himself, he slammed the door. Silence fell, and Caroline knew both of them were thinking. *What next?*

His eyes trained on her face, which was dewed with moisture and framed by a tangle of curls, Sean said slowly, 'I'd like to take you out for dinner, Caroline, I was serious about that. Are you free?'

'Yes.'

'I——' He looked down at his wet trousers legs. 'I'll drop you off at your apartment and check into a hotel. I should have done it first, I suppose, but I wanted to go straight to the bookstore. And I'll have to change and phone one of the restaurants for a reservation.'

She said in a small voice, wondering if she was being a fool but unable to help herself, 'You could change at my place.'

His voice was overly casual. 'Well, all right. If you're

sure that's okay. I could phone from there as well.' He checked the rear-view mirror and drove out of the parking lot.

'It's not very far from here. I often go walking in the park on weekends and summer evenings. In the winter there are lots of cross-country skiers, and in the summer people jog there and ride horses along the paths.' Covering her nervousness with a flood of chatter, Caroline told him a bit about the history of the park and of its fortifications. 'Oh—turn right at the stop sign and then it's the third driveway on your left.'

'Lovely old houses,' he commented. 'How many apartments in your building?'

'Four. I was really lucky to get it, the competition's fierce for these older buildings.'

They got out of the car and Caroline fumbled in her purse for her keys. Her hands were cold and not very steady; now that they were here, she was almost wishing she had taken Sean to a hotel, for once he had been inside her apartment she would never be able to view it again with quite the same eyes. She led him into the entrance hall and unlocked the door, gesturing him into the foyer. 'I'll get an old blanket for Baron,' she muttered, fleeing in the direction of the bathroom and the linen cupboard.

When she came back, blanket over her arm, Sean was still standing just inside the door. She spread the blanket on the floor and Baron collapsed on it, putting his nose on his paws with an air of being very much at home. Sean said abruptly, 'Will you show me the rest of the apartment? The rug is exquisite—it's Oriental, isn't it?'

She nodded, leading him into the living room. The apartment was very much a reflection of her own personality, and because of this she led him from room to room saying very little, feeling as though she herself was on show and wishing he would say more. However, he had seen every room, including her elegant, spacious bedroom with its rust-red chrysanthemums and cool white bedspread before he volunteered any real reaction. They were back in the living room looking out at the fog through the delicate green leaves of the fig tree, Caroline gripped by a paralysing shyness now that he was actually here in her apartment, standing only two feet away from her, the pale light of early evening falling on his deep-set eyes and thick black hair.

He said, giving another leisurely glance around the living room, 'I feel as though in five minutes I've learned a great deal more about you—your love of beauty, a need for order and harmony in your surroundings. And you're not afraid of vibrant colours, are you? Or of space . . . I can relate to that. To own things for the sake of owning them never did appeal to me, which is perhaps on reason I like sailing so much, it gets rid of all the unnecessary clutter.' He broke off, staring at her almost as if he had never seen her before. 'I lived with you for nearly three weeks, didn't I? And we made love, which is surely being as intimate as two people can be. And yet in some ways, I feel as though I scarcely know you at all.'

Caroline made an indeterminate noise. Yes, they had made love. But afterwards he had looked at her with loathing and called her Gabrielle. Wanting only to retreat from any intimacy that might make her vulnerable to more pain, she said, 'Would you like me to phone for a reservation?'

His eyes clouded. 'No, I don't want you to. Not right now. I want to make love to you again.'

'Oh, I don't think——'

He closed the distance between them, putting his arms around her. 'I want you so much, Caroline.'

'But I——'

He silenced her protest with his mouth in a kiss that seemed to Caroline to last forever. She clung to him, afraid that she would fall if she didn't, her head whirling, her whole body springing to life. Through every nerve ending she was shatteringly aware of the demands of his kiss, of the sureness of his hands roaming her body as if he had to convince himself she was real, and truly in his arms. His lips moved from her mouth to slide down the length of her throat to the pulse hammering against the smooth skin, a clue to her arousal every bit as potent as her yielding body. She was lost, she thought incoherently. Then his mouth found hers again and thought become impossible. . . .

It could have been moments or minutes before Sean swung her up into his arms and carried her through into the bedroom, pushing impatiently at the door with his shoulder, all the while raining kisses on her forehead, cheeks and hair. It was not until he laid her on the bed and almost fell on top of her, fumbling at the belt of her dress, that she was shocked back to reality.

She shoved hard at his shoulders, recognising with an hysterical urge to giggle that the nunlike dress had saved her, for both belt and zipper fastened at the back. 'Don't!' she protested, eyes wide with panic.

He lowered his full weight on her, murmuring against her face, 'It's all right, I'll be gentle with you, sweetheart. But it's been so long——'

Deaf to his reassurance, for it was not a physical assault that she feared, she tried to pull free of him, the irrational fear that possessed her giving her unexpected strength. 'I don't want you to make love to me,' she gasped. 'Sean, don't!'

His whole body grew still. He raised himself on his palms, holding himself over her, and it was as if he saw not the stark black dress or the tumble of auburn curls against the white bedspread, but only her fear-crazed eyes, huge in a face almost as white as the spread. 'What's wrong?' he demanded sharply. 'Did I hurt you?'

'No—I just don't want to make love to you, that's all.'

'You did a moment ago, I'll swear you did.'

From somewhere she managed to produce a wobbly smile. 'You're very persuasive, Sean Reilly.'

'But you don't want to be persuaded?'

'I—I'm afraid to risk it.'

'Wasn't it good for you last time?'

He was very carefully keeping emotion out of his voice, but she knew him too well to be deceived. She had hurt him. . . . She said quietly, 'It was unbelievably beautiful for me last time, Sean.'

His lashes flickered and something taut-held in the line of his mouth relaxed. 'Then what is it?'

She stared at the ceiling, knowing she had to tell him. 'It was afterwards. We went to sleep and then you woke up and called me Gabrielle, and you were—upset because you thought you'd made love to Gabrielle. Upset was too innocuous a word for the searing self-contempt she had seen in his face and that had been imprinted on her mind for ever, she knew, but it would have to do. Still not looking at him, she went on, picking her words with care, 'You see, I don't know who you made love to that day, Sean—me or Gabrielle. And for obvious reasons it makes a difference.'

'Caroline——' He cleared his throat and she glanced at his face, catching on it a look of dazed incomprehension. 'You mean . . . I called you Gabrielle? After making love to you?'

'Yes,' she whispered. 'That's the real reason I left when the Somers came. I couldn't bear to see you again.'

'Oh, God . . . no wonder!' he groaned, his head downbent so she couldn't see his face. But there was something so defeated in the curve of his shoulders that she reached up with both hands and gently pulled him down towards her. He offered no resistance, and once again she felt the warmth and weight of his body on hers.

'Who did you make love to, Sean? I have to know.'

His face was only inches from hers. 'I made love to

you, Caro,' he said, and his use of her nickname brought sudden tears to her eyes. 'I swear that, believe me. As for the other, I can't even remember it. I can't remember waking up and calling you anything, let alone Gabrielle. It doesn't sound like much of an excuse, but maybe the blow on my head was still affecting me.'

She thought back, her brow furrowed. 'You did ask me where Martin was. You wanted to know what I'd done to him. I was so hurt when you called me Gabrielle that I kind of forgot about that.'

'I could never have made love to Gabrielle. Never!'

'So—it was me?' she asked, her grammar as confused as her thoughts.

'Yes, it was you. A beautiful young woman who had come into my life as an enemy, and then who gradually started turning into someone else. Someone I couldn't despise as I despised Gabrielle, someone I started to love without even knowing who she really was. A creature of passion and laughter and a reckless kind of courage. A woman who would hold nothing back if ever she were to fall in love. That was the woman I took into my bed—I swear that, Caroline.'

'I believe you.'

There was still a painful hesitancy in his manner. 'A few moments ago I wanted to make love to you again to close the distance between us. I keep saying how strange it is to be with you again, without the shadow of Gabrielle between us. In some ways I feel as though I know you better than I've ever known anyone in my life, and yet there are so many things I don't know about you. If I could have made love to you, it would have brought you close enough that all the gaps in my knowledge wouldn't have mattered.'

'I understand.' She smiled, her lips a gentle curve. 'The zipper is at the back of my dress.'

In his eyes she saw comprehension, a swift, dazzling happiness, and the beginnings of desire chase each other

in swift succession. 'You'll have to change to go out fc
dinner anyway, won't you?' he said.

'That's true, I will. I only put this dress on because
was raining and I was feeling sorry for myself.' He
eyes, lustrous as dark satin, shone up at him with a ver
different message from the one her ordinary little word
were conveying.

He rolled off the bed and pulled her to her fee
standing behind her and for a moment putting his arm
around her and resting his chin on the top of her hea
Caroline deliberately leaned back on him, feeling hi
arms tighten their hold. She made a tiny sound c
happiness in her throat, wishing the moment could las
for ever, so perfect did it seem.

Then Sean drew back, leaving lingering kisses on th
nape of her neck as he did so. His fingers brushed he
flesh as he drew her zipper down and unsnapped th
narrow black belt at her waist. With his mouth h
traced the long curve of her spine until she shuddere
with delight. Only then did he turn her to face him
pushing the dress from her shoulders and letting it fa
in a crumpled heap on the floor. She was wearing
black slip and black lace underwear; in a swish of sil
the slip dropped to the floor as well.

Caroline's heart was thumping so loudly she wa
sure he would be able to hear it. Trying to soun
casual but not quite succeeding, she said, 'Your turn
as she tugged his sweater out of his waistband an
eased it up over his ribs. He shrugged out of i
bringing her hands to his chest and holding ther
there so she could feel the heavy pounding of his ow
heart, and then letting them slide to his waist t
unbuckle his trousers. The rest of his clothes, and th
skimpy wisps of lace that were hers, joined the othe
garments on the floor.

His body was as lean and elegant as an ancien
statue; when he stepped closer to her so that the
touched at breast and hip and knee, she was trembling

her eyes the dark, impenetrable purple of pansies, on her cheeks the pink of wild rose petals. He kissed her, and she respondered joyously and generously, all the love that was in her wanting to give him as much pleasure as he was giving her. This time when he lifted her on to the bed, there were no protests; she simply opened her arms to him, offering him lips and body without reserve.

He kissed her long and deeply, his hands caressing the silken fullness of her breasts, all the force and passion of his manhood throbbing against her thigh; it was a triple assault to which she freely succumbed, a yielding that was at the same time a gift of all her own passionate need of him.

They made love without words, his stormy grey eyes sensitive to her every move as with hands and lips he judged her arousal, intent upon delighting her and tormenting her with all the nuances of desire. Not until her hips were writhing under him and she was moaning for release did his shuddering body find its home in her, arrow to the gold; in his own surrender, he became victor and conquerer, and her one fierce cry of joy was a paean to that shared victory and shared surrender.

He collapsed against her, his back running with sweat, his breath shaking in his throat, and Caroline held him so close that her own heartbeat raced against his ribs. Suffused with contentment and peace, she did not think she could ever be happier. But she was wrong, for Sean said huskily, cupping her face in his hands and looking deep into her eyes, 'I love you so much, Caroline. I don't think I'll ever have enough of you.'

'You—what?' she croaked incredulously, wondering if she was dreaming.

'I love you. Love you, love you, love you. . . .' With each word he nibbled at her earlobe, his eyes filled with tenderness. 'I didn't mean to say anything yet. I meant

to give you time, let you get used to the idea that it'
you, Caroline, whom I want for the rest of my life an
love more than I thought it possible to love anyone. Bu
I can't help telling you.'

'You really mean it?' she said stupidly.

He began to laugh. 'How many times do I have t
repeat it? I love you, Caroline.'

'But——'

She was about to say *I love you, too*. However, h
pressed one finger against her lips, the laughter fleein
from his face. 'I hope in time you'll come to feel th
same way—you don't know how much I hope and lon
for that. But how can I expect you to love me when
treated you the way I did? Locking you up because
hated everything you stood for. Ignoring you for hour
at a time because all you did was remind me of Martin
Setting Baron on you . . . I still shudder when I think o
that!'

Impatiently Caroline pulled his hand away from he
lips, but before she could say anything he kissed her, a
slow gentle kiss of caring and commitment rather tha
of passion. 'There's hope for me,' he murmured agains
her mouth. 'You wouldn't have made love to me unles
you at least wanted me physically, would you
Caroline?' Without letting her answer, he began kissin
her again. She pushed him away, her eyes brimming wit
laughter and with an emotion that made his breat
catch in his throat. 'Caroline——'

'I love you, too,' she cried. 'You just wouldn't kee
quiet long enough for me to tell you.' Happiness bega
to dawn in his face, a happiness beyond anything sh
had ever seen before, and his features blurred as tear
crowded her eyes. 'How could I help loving you?' sh
quavered, adding unromantically, 'Oh, Sean, you are a
idiot—didn't you know?'

'Of course not.'

'Why do you think I was so hurt when you called m
Gabrielle? It was because I was hopelessly in love wit

you, and you wouldn't even acknowledge that I existed.'

He said grimly, 'I knew that you existed all right. Not right away, when I first took you to the Somers'. I was too blinded by hatred and a need for vengeance to know who you were then. But all too soon the woman I'd only met that once in a night club and the woman I'd brought to Deep River came into conflict. It was the little things at first. Your love of the opera and of the outdoors. The kind of reading you did. Your stoicism when you burned your arm. The night I met Gabrielle we were dancing when someone stepped on her toe—quite hard, mind you, but not nearly hard enough to justify the fuss she made. And Gabrielle wouldn't listen to *Aida*. Punk rock's more her line.'

He ran his fingers through his hair, his eyes lost in remembrance. 'But it was more than that. There's an inward honesty about you that I felt had to be real. Yet how could it be real when I knew you'd lied and stolen and cheated? I sensed a fire and passion in you that Gabrielle never had . . . yet all I could conclude was that you were a superb actress. And your laughter. . . .' He kissed her hard. 'I adore the way you laugh, it's all part of your love of life, isn't it? Gabrielle doesn't know how to laugh like that.'

'Poor Gabrielle,' Caroline said involuntarily.

'Yes, poor Gabrielle.' He grinned crookedly. 'But back at the Somers' it was poor me. I felt as though I was going crazy, Caroline. You *had* to be Gabrielle. And yet more and more I saw a different woman, and it was with that woman that I began to fall in love. It was almost as though history was repeating itself. Martin had been in love with Gabrielle, and now I was falling in love with a woman who looked like Gabrielle, who had been in one of the villages where I'd expected to find Gabrielle, and yet who was different from Gabrielle. There were days I thought I would go mad if

I didn't resolve it one way or the other. Gabrielle o
Caroline. A woman I loathed and a woman I wa
beginning to love in spite of all the dictates of cautio
and rationality.' He hesitated, his face bleak. 'All m
instincts told me you were real, honest and true and ful
of gaiety and courage. You were the other half of me
the woman I'd been subconsciously waiting for all m
life.'

'I feel the same way about you. Without you I'n
incomplete.'

'And then, the day of the storm, instead of runnin
away as you had every opportunity to do, you staye
and rescued me. So it was Caroline I made love to
because it was she who had the bravery and the stamin
to haul me from the boat to the house in the middle o
a hurricane.'

'And who then disappeared immediately after
wards,' she supplied wryly. 'What *did* you tell th
Somers?'

'I told them to mind their own bloody business an
get me to a doctor. Ian took it in his stride. Joan, o
course, kept asking all kinds of awkward questions tha
I couldn't—or wouldn't—answer. Glad I'm not goin
to marry someone like her.'

'Oh? Are you planning to marry someone?' Carolin
asked demurely.

Sean looked down at her naked body nestled s
closely to his and said calmly, 'I think I'd bette
marry you.'

'I think you'd better, too.'

'Make an honest woman out of you.'

She giggled. 'I know that's the only reason.'

He raised his eyebrows. 'What other reason coul
there possibly be?' Then he ruined his own rhetoric b
adding fiercely, 'You will marry me, won't you
Caroline? Because I love you and I don't think I ca
live without you.'

'Yes, Sean, I'll marry you.' Her heart in her eyes, sh

reached up and kissed him, and for a few moments there was silence.

Then, against her cheek, Sean murmured, 'We'd better get up and go to dinner. Or else you're going to be overtaken by a fate worse than death.'

'Sounds like fun,' she said wickedly.

'You're an insatiable woman. What's the name of a good restaurant?'

'I forget.'

'I can take a hint.' He brought both hands to her breasts and began stroking them, so that her whole body quivered with delight.

This time they made love more slowly, beginning to learn what pleased each other and asking the intimate little questions that only lovers share. But the culmination was as irrevocable, as powerful, and as agonisingly beautiful as before.

They slept for a while, waking to find that it was already dark. Sean said firmly, although Caroline could hear the smile in his voice, 'We're going out for something to eat, Caroline Travers.'

'Yes, Sean,' she answered obediently.

'And you will wear a dress other than that black one.'

'Yes, Sean.' She chuckled. 'But only because I want to. I wouldn't want you to think I'll be one of those meek and mild housewives who kowtow to their husband's every wish.'

'I'm not the slightest bit worried about that possibility.'

'I just wanted to keep the record straight. After all, you started off thinking I was someone other than I was.'

'I won't make that mistake again.' His arm tightened around her. 'Because now I know who you are, Caroline, and I love the woman I know you to be.'

She ran her fingers up his chest, tangling them

in the dark hair, her voice shaken with the intensity of her feelings. 'I love you, too, Sean.'

After that, of course, it was some time before they left the apartment; they arrived at the restaurant only ten minutes before it closed.

Harlequin Plus

A WORD ABOUT THE AUTHOR

Born in England, Sandra Field today makes her home in Nova Scotia, Canada. Converts, she says, are usually fanatical in their new beliefs, and Sandra is strongly attached to the Maritimes, with its sometimes inhospitable climate but breathtakingly beautiful scenery.

She has lived in all three of Canada's maritime provinces, but it was during her stay on tiny Prince Edward Island, where the beaches are legendary but the winters long, that she first decided to write a book. The local library provided her with a guide for aspiring authors, and she followed the instructions to a "t."

It was no simple job, she recalls now. In fact, a major crisis occurred when she ran out of plot several thousand words short of the mark! But eventually she completed it, to the delight of her readers. The book was *To Trust My Love* (Romance #1870), published in 1975.

Her many interests, which she likes to weave into her stories, include birdwatching, studying wild flowers and participating in such winter activities as snowshoeing and cross-country skiing. She particularly enjoys classical music, especially that of the Romantic period.

Enter a uniquely exciting new world with

Harlequin American Romance™

Harlequin American Romances are the first romances to explore today's love relationships. These compelling novels reach into the hearts and minds of women across America... probing the most intimate moments of romance, love and desire.

You'll follow romantic heroines and irresistible men as they boldly face confusing choices. Career first, love later? Love without marriage? Long-distance relationships? All the experiences that make love real are captured in the tender, lovin' pages of **Harlequin American Romances.**

What makes American women so different when it comes to love? Find out with **Harlequin American Romance!**

Send for your introductory FREE book now!

Get this book FREE!

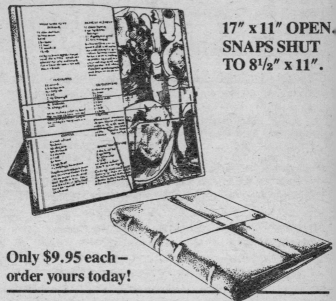